Christine A. Schimpf

Finding His Way Home

Christine A. Schimpf

Finding His Way Home by Christine Schimpf, Member of Faith, Hope & Love Christian Writers

Blessed are those who hunger and thirst for righteousness, for they shall be filled.

Matthew 5:6

Copyright © 2024 by Christine A. Schimpf

Published by Forget Me Not Romances, an imprint of Winged Publications

Editor: Cynthia Hickey
Book Design by Winged Publications

All rights reserved. No part of this publication may be reproduced, stored in a retrieval system, or transmitted in any form or by any means—electronic, mechanical, photocopying, recording, or otherwise—without the prior written permission of the publisher. The only exception is brief quotations in printed reviews. Piracy is illegal. Thank you for respecting the hard work of this author.

This book is a work of fiction. Names, characters, Places, incidents, and dialogues are either products of the author's imagination or used fictitiously. Any resemblance to actual persons, living or dead, or events is coincidental.

ISBN-13: 979-8-3303-0904-7

Dedication
To my critique ladies…Katie, Andrea, Cat and Rosemary.
Thank you for sticking with me all these years. I couldn't have done it without you.

Chapter 1

Roman Hart craved change.

He pulled the nail he'd pinched between his lips and pounded it into the last strip of aluminum siding onto the clubhouse. He rested his hands on his hips and scanned the golf course he'd worked as a course consultant and maintenance professional for the last couple of months. He was pleased the job was done and all he'd accomplished. As usual, he was anxious to get a head start on the next job.

"Bob, that wraps it up. You're all set for the upcoming season," Roman said to the Whispering Shores Golf Course manager, who had just walked over and was eyeing Roman's work.

The course manager drew a long swallow from the plastic bottle of diet cola he enjoyed every morning in place of coffee. Roman still couldn't figure that one out. He'd prefer a hot cup of coffee any day of the week over soda.

"We couldn't have done this without you, Roman." Bob stuck out his hand and the two men shook. "Where you off to?"

Roman glanced at his watch. "Sister Bay. There's a club over there that needs some help. I'm expecting a call with more details later this morning."

"Love the public beach over there. If you can, sit down and enjoy the view, although you don't look the type that relaxes much." Bob harrumphed, then took another swig.

Roman chuckled. Bob was right. Working for his uncle and partner as a golf course consultant across the Midwest for the last decade kept him jumping from one job to the next. Just the way he liked it. In the off-season, he kept himself busy by taking on maintenance work or making follow-up appointments with his clients. Even though he didn't mind the challenges of the consulting side, he still preferred hard labor. Working with his hands on lawn maintenance, repairing sprinkler systems, and reseeding greens was more his preference. Walking a course, breathing the fresh air, and feeling the warm sun on his face was a soothing balm for his troubled soul.

As usual, Roman was eager to hit the road. Each new job was a challenge for him, viewing the problems like a huge obstacle course to get through to the finish line. With the job complete, Roman slipped his hammer into his tool belt. "If you need a follow-up in the fall, just call." He instructed Bob.

"Will do. Thanks again, Roman."

Roman jogged down the short flight of stairs that led to the parking lot, ignoring the needling pain in his bad foot. He headed to his truck and drove west toward Sister Bay. A couple of hours later, with some time to kill, he rolled through the downtown area, trying to refresh his memory, taking it all in. He intended to squeeze in a quick, hot breakfast, but when he spotted the local hardware store, he changed his mind. He loved checking out the new lawn equipment, examining the electric power tools, and glancing at the synthetic oil. It always put a smile on his face. Maybe he was a simple man, but there was peace in knowing who he was. A hard day's work brought him back to his center and calmed him, keeping his past mistakes at bay.

Stepping out of the vehicle he winced with the first couple of steps on his bad foot, a constant reminder of the biggest mistake of his life. Inside his boot, he stretched his toes before each step as he walked toward the store, easing the tightness from the screws that held the tiny bones together. He thrust his hands deep into his jacket pockets. The wind coming off the Bay was crisp this morning. He breathed in the fresh air. Roman reached for the door but stopped his stride, hearing his phone ring. A photo of his uncle at the last Christmas gathering lit up the screen. *He's right on time.*

"Roman, I'm sure I don't have to ask how you're doing because I already know you're ripped and ready to go." Roman smiled, hearing the hearty laugh coming from the man he regarded as his second father.

Even though the choppy water of the Bay was uninviting, Roman turned from the store and headed toward a cedar-plank park bench that offered a view of the public beach to take the call.

Roman flipped up the collar on his coat. "I'm checking out the business district."

"Let me guess. Is there a hardware store in your sights?" Uncle Jake harrumphed.

Roman heard the humor in his uncle's question. He lifted his gaze to the sky. He was found out once again.

"Listen, Roman, before you head over to the job, I want to clue you in on what's going on over there."

Roman heard the lift in Uncle Jake's voice and knew exactly what that meant. His uncle had taken an active role in the search for a golf course that Roman's pocketbook could afford. Roman's adrenaline spiked. "Is it for sale?"

"Hold on. Hold on. Not quite, but, uh, maybe." His uncle's warning tone carried a heavy note of caution.

Roman's steamroll approach to life lost momentum. "What does that mean, exactly?"

"I had a conversation yesterday with an old friend of mine, Bill Moros."

Roman counted to ten in his head, praying for patience. "Go on." He rose from the bench and started a trek toward the water. The wind coming off the Bay slapped at his cheeks. Why hadn't he grabbed his scarf? "And?"

"His business partner passed on and left his shares of Cherry Orchard Golf Course to his grandkids. It's not in good shape for a myriad of reasons and has been losing money for the last several years."

"Do the grandkids want to sell?"

"That's the tricky part. I'm not sure, but that's what Bill would like. He's the majority shareholder. He said the kids may want to give it a go first for sentimental reasons."

Roman's balloon of hope deflated as fast as his excitement had gained momentum. Warning bells went off in his head. *Be careful here. This is not an ideal situation.* Was he about to check off another course from the mental list in his head? "Hmm. Sounds messy. I think I'll pass on this one. What else do you have?"

"Hey. I wouldn't be so quick to write this one off just yet. This is prime real estate in Wisconsin's Door County. I'm sure you've been there, but you might not remember what it's known as."

His uncle was right. He remembered a family trip or two over to Sister Bay but nothing stuck out to him right now. "Remind me," Roman grumbled, preferring to hear the details of another job. He didn't want to waste his time investing in a dead end.

"The Cape Cod of the Midwest. Gets millions of visitors every year. I get the vibe that Bill doesn't have much faith in the next generation. Who knows, maybe they'd sell, especially if you make them an offer they can't refuse."

Maybe he should lift his foot off his skepticism. His uncle's instincts were usually sound, and he trusted his advice. *Is this the one, Lord?* How long had he waited for this moment? He rounded the pier and started back to the park bench. With the wind now at his back, he heard the waves slap against the rocks. As the village came back into view, an inviting warmth enveloped him.

The scene was cozy, like that of a *Hallmark* greeting card, with clapboard shops that lined the streets and American flags flapping in the wind. Black-gray smoke curled from shops' chimneys. A cafe offered a hot coffee and croissant special, causing his stomach to rumble. His gaze breezed past a bookstore and a couple of restaurants to the top of the hill and landed on a bowling alley. He used to love throwing a ball down an oil-slicked alley. He'd have to visit the place if he stuck around. The village had made a good first impression on him. He liked the place. A lot. Maybe he should give this golf course a visit. What could it hurt?

Roman heard a file drawer close with a bang, drawing him back to the conversation with his uncle. "I've got the address here somewhere," Jake said. "Wait a minute. Hold on. Here we go. This is when I wished you used the text option on your phone."

Roman clenched his teeth. He'd never text again. Not after suffering the consequences the last time he did. "Not happening in this lifetime."

Jake exhaled out a moan. "I get it. I'll send it to your email. You've got a meeting tomorrow morning over there with one of the grandkids. Ask for Alex. If you don't get a good vibe, call me and you can push on to the next job. But if this club is what I think it is, it could be your diamond in the rough. You go for it and get that program of yours up and running."

The program…Roman's dream became his mission shortly after the accident…to pilot a golf program for teens and those headed down the wrong path. The same path he'd taken so many years ago. He could finally cleanse his conscience and make up for all the suffering he had caused to so many people he loved. It meant the world to him, but the key was finding a course he could afford so the program could get a start. He trusted his uncle's insights. Maybe this was the one. He retrieved his notepad and pen from his back pocket and took down the details. "I agree. It's worth a look. I'll let you know how it pans out."

"And Roman?"

"Yeah?"

"Stay out of the hardware store. I've got a notion you don't need more tools," Jake chuckled.

With a grin plastered on his face, Roman pushed the door open to the hardware store and walked in.

Roman heard the ding-dong overhead alerting the staff another customer had entered.

"Hello, and welcome to Village Hardware," one of the checkout clerks said. "Looking for anything special?"

Roman slid his sunglasses to the top of his head. He didn't intend to shop but to browse and take a mental inventory. Now sharing in his uncle's enthusiasm, he gestured and said, "I'm good, thanks."

Reading the aisle signs overhead, he passed a large display of thermoses, then stopped short of nearly running into a life-sized poster of a very attractive woman dressed in jeans and a cotton shirt with rolled-up cuffs. *What a show-stopper.* With a ponytail sticking out of a baseball cap, she held a drill that just happened to be his favorite brand.

Roman swallowed a laugh when he heard footsteps drawing near.

"May I help you?"

Roman jerked his head toward the voice. He glanced back at the poster, then at the employee standing next to him, and back at the poster again—same blue eyes. Same golden hair pulled back loosely into a ponytail. He liked the flannel shirt she wore tucked into a pair of fitted jeans and Toughie work boots on her feet. "You make it look easy," Roman said, nodding to the poster.

Her eyes narrowed. "I get that reaction a lot."

Roman thumbed at the cardboard clone. "Do you have a knack for power tools, or is this all just a marketing ploy to get suckers like me to buy?"

She lifted her hand. "It's no joke. Instead of dolls, I played with a tool bench when I was little. What can I say?"

Roman grinned. "I can't argue with that, so did I."

"Are you interested in taking a look at the recent additions in the line?"

Roman threw his shoulders back, straightening his six-foot frame. "I believe I am. I have a good feeling that things are finally going to work out for me today."

Her eyes widened. "Sounds like big plans. No wonder you're grinning from ear to ear."

Not only attractive but funny.

"This line is one of our best sellers. Reliable. Durable. Dependable," she explained.

Roman thumbed at the poster. "And wouldn't you know, it's my favorite brand?"

When she released a laugh, Roman didn't think the morning could get any better, but it just did.

Roman followed the scent of her cherry blossom perfume as she made her way to one of the last aisles. It was no surprise they'd selected her for the poster. They'd sell plenty of tools.

His heart picked up beats as he noticed the wide selection. It would be hard for him to resist purchasing one of these babies right now. Despite what his uncle said, he could always beef up his repertoire of gadgets.

"So, you're new in town?" she asked. The look in her eyes and the honey tone in her voice matched his impression of the village, warm, friendly, and inviting. He hoped she worked at this store location. Running into her from time to time would be a pleasure.

Roman couldn't contain his excitement. "I might be, but that all depends on how the day unfolds. I'm in the market for a golf course."

Her eyebrows lifted, revealing a splattering of

freckles sprinkled across her nose. He'd always liked freckles and thought they were cute.

"Sounds promising," she said.

Roman couldn't tell if she was asking him a question or simply stating a fact. He chose to clarify. "Not really, just uncertain at the moment. Are you from the area?" Roman forced his gaze from the attractive woman to the electric weed eaters. Women had a way of distracting him and this situation was no exception. He'd be smart to remember he had a meeting to go to.

"Born and raised and there's no place I'd rather be." Her tone was unmistakably clear. She loved the place, and he could understand why. It had a charm that was hard to find. Traveling all over the Midwest made him a bit of an expert in nice places to live.

A request for a manager made its way across the store over the intercom system. It interrupted their conversation and Roman's brewing idea for a cup of coffee later. He enjoyed her quick wit and sense of humor. She was also an attractive woman that he'd like to get to know better, especially if he'd be sticking around.

"I need to answer that call, so I'll leave you to it. We're here to help if you need it; although, you did say this was your *favorite* line." The dimples in her cheeks deepened with her smile.

Roman watched her walk away. *So, she's a manager.*

~

Thirty minutes later, Roman leaned against his pickup and pulled up the address on the navigation app on his phone. He had to get moving to make the meeting.

"Are you lost?"

It was her. He recognized her voice. When he looked over his shoulder at the woman approaching, his heart skipped a beat. Her honey-colored hair fell across her shoulders after losing the ponytail. *Striking.*

Roman turned toward her. "No, just trying to find the best route to where I need to be tomorrow."

"I've lived here all my life. I can probably help you out. Where are you going?" Her gaze drifted to his phone. Eyelashes, the same color as her hair, fluttered to protect her eyes against a gust of wind.

"Cherry Orchard Golf Course."

Her smile broadened and her cheeks colored a pretty shade of pink.

Pulling a loose strand of hair aside from her face, she said, "I spent a lot of time there as a child. It's one of the area's unique golfing experiences."

Roman winced. "It may have been at one time, but I'm told they're in some serious trouble now. They could very well end up on the chopping block."

The captivating smile from a moment ago had disappeared as swiftly as the clouds overhead blocked the sun. Roman was no longer looking into a pair of warm and friendly eyes but those straight out of the cold ocean blue.

Uh-oh. What did I say?

"Take Highway 40 to Landings Edge Road and make a right. Cherry Orchard will come into view," she instructed in a tight voice. She turned and stomped off without a goodbye or a farewell, or *I hope you make it to your destination.*

Hmm. Taken aback, Roman shook his head, trying to make sense of what had just happened. He had never had a problem communicating before. *What did I say?*

Her Jeep turned out of the parking lot, kicking up loose gravel in her wake.

Frustrated, he didn't have time to figure out what just happened or he *would* be late for the meeting. He crammed his phone into his back pocket and climbed into his truck.

I guess that squashes any hope of a date down the road.

Shaking his head in disappointment, he blew out a sigh. *Too bad.*

Chapter 2

Lexi Russo stepped onto the eighteenth green at Cherry Orchard Golf Course, always preferring to walk and use a pushcart rather than ride in a golf cart. With a view of the Bay, she paused, listening to the sounds of the waves crashing into the shoreline. Heavy clouds dragged overhead. Even Mother Nature was mourning the loss of her grandfather, their family's patriarch. With her next breath, she closed her eyes, picking up the subtle scent of evergreen in the spring air. Every wonderful moment in her life was experienced right here. Not at home, where her father ignored her. Here, at her grandfather's side. *Now* she understood why he'd chosen *her* to run his course after his death. *I won't let you down.*

    Lexi exhaled a heavy sigh. She was uncomfortable in her grandfather's shoes. She knew inheriting the golf course, along with her two sisters, in Door County, Wisconsin, would come at a price. With her older sister, Analise, finishing up her last semester in law school and her younger sister, Elliana, busy as an interior decorator, every task, both large and small, would fall on her shoulders. Allowing her worst fears to gain traction in her heart, she wondered if Gramps had chosen the wrong granddaughter for operations manager. Her thoughts drifted back to that awful conversation she'd had with that brazen man in the parking lot. Attractive or not, when he told her that Cherry Orchard could very well end up on the chopping block, she could've spit nails. The nerve of him. Ugh! Lexi shivered at the idea of selling the beloved course.

Lexi grabbed her putter, sensing the calm that always filled her. Most players tensed up when they reached the green. Not her, not ever. Gramps had told her it was because she had a special gift with the putter. He was right. Golf always had a way of clearing her head and setting her mind straight. Lexi studied the green's slope, found her target, and lined up the striking side of the putter to the hole. *Line it up with the sweet spot*, Gramps told her. How many times? Lexi couldn't remember. Spreading her fingers, she placed her hands on the shaft of the club. Her thumbs slid easily into position as if grooved into the grip. Judging the distance to the hole with a tuned eye, she moved her shoulders back and through the swing. The hollow *kerplunk* told her she sank the putt.

"Yes!" Lexi pumped a fist into the air. It felt good to play again.

The familiar burst of adrenaline coursed through her. Working at the hardware store for the last few years had her grinding out ten-hour days, six days a week to earn the title of manager. She was no stranger to doing what it took to succeed. *Will this new experience be just what I need?*

After retrieving her ball from the hole, she slipped the head cover on the club and returned the putter to her golf bag. As always, she recorded her score and then followed the cherry tree line back to the clubhouse. Small buds were noticeable on the trees, but as soon as the weather warmed, their blossoms would speckle the limbs. How many pictures had they taken along this path? She picked up her pace, not wanting to be late for the party today. Everyone was coming, and it'd be good to see her sisters again.

"I thought I'd find you here." Lexi's older sister, Analise, pulled Lexi out of her daydreaming. She waited on the worn cedar wrap-around deck. Lexi noticed the wear from the previous heavy snow winter. She made a mental note to add stain to her list and the deck project as another task to complete before the season opener.

Lexi smiled at the sight of her sibling. She'd missed her these last couple of months since the funeral. The law school she attended in Milwaukee kept her busy and her visits infrequent. Now that Analise was in her last semester, Lexi hoped she'd move back to Door County after she passed the bar exam.

"It's the best way to start the day." The lump in Lexi's throat was immediate as she repeated their grandfather's mantra for life.

Analise's eyes softened. "The apple sure doesn't fall far from the tree, does it?"

Lexi knew her sister didn't expect an answer to that question but heard her grandfather's reminiscent advice echo in her head. "Look at the grass, Lex. See how it bends toward the sun? That's going to play into how the ball responds to the putt."

As Lexi grew older, their conversations became more serious. How the rough had to be cultivated for a challenge, but not frustration. How the sand bunkers needed to be maintained to test a player's ability, and how to use the water to create a distraction. He'd been grooming her all along for this moment.

She steered her attention back to her sister. "Is Nana here yet?"

Analise zipped up her fleece-lined jacket against the snappy April wind. "She's in the dining room talking with the staff. They're swarming around her like little bees. She's in heaven. Ellie's there too."

"Perfect. All I have to do is find the matches and light the candles for her birthday cake."

When Analise filled her lungs with the crisp April air, Lexi knew bad news was coming.

"I have something I'd like to talk to you about. It involves good news and not so good," Analise said.

Lexi picked up on Analise's insistence. Something was up. Lexi could hear it in her voice. "I can't imagine anything more important than celebrating Nana's seventy-fifth birthday." Lexi almost wished whatever was coming would disappear.

"You will after I tell you what's going on. I got a call from Uncle Bill last night."

Bill Moros was hardly their uncle, but he had been a close friend and business partner of their grandfather's. When Gramps introduced him as their uncle, the title stuck. He was also the majority shareholder of the golf course. Lexi's instincts warned her that this would be the unpleasant part of their conversation, although she couldn't imagine why. Gramps's relationship with Uncle Bill was steadfast right up until his death. "I hope this is the good news part."

Analise shook her head. "Not so much. He didn't want to spring this on us so close to the reading of the will, but he couldn't put it off any longer. He wants to retire and sell his shares. A developer who's very interested in the property has approached him, but he'd rather sell to us, of course."

Lexi threw up her hands. "I appreciate that he's giving us first rights to buy his shares, but the timing! It's not the best news, especially now."

Analise shook her head. "No, it isn't."

"Should we go inside? I think Ellie needs to be a part of this conversation." With a practiced hand, Lexi opened the door gingerly to avoid dislodging the loose screws on the hinge. She made a mental note to replace them tomorrow before the whole door came down.

She heard her sister's footsteps right behind her as they stepped into the small work kitchen. "Can we talk about this after the party? I'm sure Nana is getting antsy for her birthday celebration."

When Analise crossed her arms, Lexi knew this was serious. "I don't want to keep Nana waiting either, Lex, but this is something we need to figure out."

"Now you're scaring me. How serious is this?"

"It's not something we can't handle and if I could stay after the party I would, but I need to get back to school. Law students never sleep, remember? Despite all the teasing I gave Ellie, I'm glad she never moved from the area. She'll be a lot closer than I will be in case you need her."

"Me too," Lexi said. "But I'm not letting you off the hook that easy. Once you get your law degree, I hope you come home, so we can all be together again." The idea of recreating a sense of family meant the world to Lexi. Even if that family were just her and her sisters. After their father remarried and started a new family and their mother moved to Costa Rica, it felt as if they were floating on a life raft on Lake Michigan without a mooring.

Analise crossed her fingers, wishing for good luck. "If I can land a job close by, that's the plan."

"Does Ellie know yet?" Lexi asked.

Before Analise could answer the question, the door between the dining room and kitchen swung open. Ellie entered the room. "Know what?"

"That Uncle Bill wants to sell his shares, and he'd like us to buy them," Analise said.

Ellie's eyes grew wide. "What does that mean for us?"

Lexi grew silent, already knowing the answer to Ellie's question.

"Uncle Bill has a controlling interest. If he sells to an outsider, we could lose Cherry Orchard," Analise said, unknowingly igniting a fear deep inside Lexi. She couldn't let that happen. This was her safe place in the world. The only place she ever wanted to be. Some of her friends moved away after college or married someone who moved them for a career. Lexi wanted none of that.

"Surely, he'll listen to reason." The panic in Ellie's rising voice made Lexi's heart soften. She was the spitfire among them, rolling on the highs and lows of her emotions, creating havoc and joy at the same time in all of their lives.

Lexi knew keeping Ellie calm was key. Using a leveled voice, she asked, "Is he willing to give us some time to figure this all out?"

Analise grimaced. "I asked Uncle Bill for his timeline. He agreed to give us one more season."

"One more season? But that's next month." Ellie's voice neared screechy, a telltale sign she was growing upset.

"Keep your voice down or Nana will be the next one to walk into this room and the surprise will be ruined," Lexi warned.

Ellie raised her hands. "Sorry. With all this going on, I forgot all about the party. But this is the last thing we need right now," she grumbled.

Lexi nibbled on her bottom lip. "You're right. Not only do we need to make course repairs and updates to the clubhouse, but now have to worry about turning over a profit to buy Uncle Bill's shares."

"We need a knight in shining armor to accomplish all of that," Ellie suggested, wearing a grin.

Despite their circumstances, Lexi and Analise chuckled. If only it were that easy, Lexi thought. Her grandfather would tell her not to worry, and that all things work together for God's good. Thank goodness she had faith she could rely on that would sustain her through all of this.

Lexi shivered and then pulled her sweater tight around her waist. "Let's not blame Uncle Bill for wanting to step into his future. That wouldn't be fair. It is a problem, but we can figure it out, with or without Ellie's knight in shining armor." Lexi gave her youngest sister a wink.

"You're right," Ellie said.

"We can handle this," Analise said, then laid a hand on her chest. "We're three educated, strong, independent women. Gramps wouldn't have passed down what was most dear to him if he didn't believe in our capabilities."

A thought bombarded Lexi's thoughts. She knew it would break their Nana's heart to lose this place too. Losing her husband was enough. "Not a word to Nana."

Her sisters' response was immediate. "Agreed," Ellie and Analise said.

"With all of this going on, now I'm sorry that I can't be here to help, but finals are coming up fast." The look on Analise's face turned apologetic.

Ellie raised a hand. "Don't be silly. You need to finish your education strong. We can take care of this, right Lex?"

Lexi nodded. "We have a ton of maintenance issues, but nothing that can't be fixed."

"We all know that Gramps didn't keep up with repairs the last few years."

"Elliana was right. Their grandfather had allowed the course to wither on the vine a bit, but Lexi had no intention of letting it die, despite her doubts that she wasn't qualified for the job.

"It's just finding that person who can do the fixing. I know you think you can do it all, Lex, but you're going to need help, and I've got a full-time job at the design center," Ellie's point was loud and clear.

"There is a sizable amount of cash in the account for repair work. We could put an ad in the paper for a handyman." Analise suggested.

Lexi's heart bottomed out. She knew improvements had to be made, but the thought of hiring a professional didn't sit well. "I don't want to change too much or we'll lose the essence of Cherry Orchard." Memories when she and Gramps savored grilled cheese and pickle sandwiches while they watched the installers lay the new flooring flooded her thoughts. Hands on his hips, he was so pleased when they'd finished the job.

"We don't have to figure it all out right now," Analise said.

Lexi forced a smile. Analise always had been the leader among them. Somehow, her calm approach acted as a healing salve on the wound of change, heading in their direction.

"You're right," Lexi said. "Let me ask around about a handyman and if I don't have any luck I'll start a search. For now, let's remember why we're all here."

"We have a 75th birthday person to honor," Ellie said.

"Why don't you light those candles so we can get out there and wish Nana a happy birthday?" Analise suggested, hitting the sweet spot among them.

Lexi placed the cake on a serving platter, lit the candles, and then started toward the dining room. Analise held the door and Ellie would follow behind. A warmth so powerful filled her as much as that last putt she'd made, knowing how happy Gramps would have been about that little achievement. How many celebrations had they held here over the years? Lexi made a silent vow. No matter what, she'd make sure their traditions would live on, even if she wasn't quite sure how she'd pull it all off. Inhaling a deep breath, she launched into song with her sisters. "Happy birthday to you. Happy birthday to you."

Lexi squeezed back the tears fighting the fear that this could very well be the last family party they would enjoy together at Cherry Orchard.

Chapter 3

The next morning, Roman pulled up to Cherry Orchard Golf Course. From his seat in the pickup truck, he eyed the worn shingles on the roof, the woodpecker holes in the cedar siding, and the weeds peeking through the cracked concrete in the parking lot. It told him what he came to see. The place needed a lot of work. He assumed the inside wasn't much better by the looks of the windows that needed replacement. It was perfect. His uncle's words of encouragement echoed in his head. *This may be the one.*

Turning off the truck, he carefully dropped his feet to the ground. *Well, Lord, let's go have a look.* He took slow, methodical steps at first, allowing his bad foot to warm up, as he called it, and made his way to the clubhouse. His gaze moved like a magnet to the water. A line of cherry trees hugged the southern edge of the course. He slowed his steps as he took in a spectacular view. Of all the golf facilities he'd worked on over the years, this one, by far, had a rare quality…charm. He'd bet his last paycheck developers were hovering, lying in wait to scoop up such a beautiful property. A bitter taste tainted Roman's tongue with the thought of a conglomeration of condos in its place.

As he turned the corner of the building, a woman dressed in jeans and a cotton T-shirt caught his attention. He found her on her knees, working on the bottom hinge of the entrance door. Golden hair peeked out of a baseball cap, reminding him of the poster girl at the hardware store. He sure wished that situation would've ended differently.

With each whirl of the drill, the top hinge loosened from the door frame. *It was probably rotted out.* The hinge freed up, and the door pulled away from the frame, heading straight for him.

Fast.

Roman bolted forward and grabbed the falling door with two firm hands. "Whoa. Looks like you could use a little help here."

"What? Oh, no!" She scrambled out from under the door and rose to face him.

Roman couldn't help but stare. It looked like…no…it was… the attractive woman in the poster…and the parking lot. Trying to put the pieces together, he finally asked, "You work *here* too?"

"I own it," she said without a smile, "along with my two sisters. I'm Lexi Russo."

"Ah," Roman tilted his head while noticing the daggers in her eyes. Lexi as in Alex as in Alexandria. He hadn't expected to meet a woman, especially not *this* woman. Why hadn't his uncle told him he'd be meeting with the granddaughter and not the grandson?

"And you're the man from the hardware store

interested in electrical tools."

He nodded. "Yes, I'm Roman Hart. I want to apologize if I gave the wrong impression back there." He felt like a heel for saying what he did. If he had known who she was, he would have buttoned his lips and swallowed down his opinion. "I hope you'll give me another chance."

Narrowing her eyes, Lexi asked, "To do what? Buy my golf course? Is this the place you were hoping would work out for you today?"

"Ah..." Again, a loss for words. What was it about this woman that had him tongue-tied? He had a pitch all set in his head, the one his uncle had told him to craft, but he couldn't seem to retrieve a single word of it. Roman raised defensive hands. "Let me explain."

Lexi placed the drill on a side table with a loud thump while Roman leaned the door against the building, scrambling to come up with something.

Hands now on her hips, she gave him her full attention. "Oh, yes, please do."

"I've worked for the last ten years in golf course maintenance and have done some consulting. And, yes, I admit, I'm always in the market for a gently used course, but more importantly, I have a program for kids that I'm trying to launch. That's really my heart's passion and the reason for my search."

Roman's last words seemed to catch the woman's attention. She tilted her head at him and when the afternoon sun washed over her face. He noticed her high cheekbones, smooth skin, and a soft tilt on her lips. She was a beautiful woman and one that meant business.

"But you meant what you said back there in the parking lot. That Cherry Orchard could be on the chopping block."

Roman opened his mouth to counter but knew he couldn't sidestep his way out of that comment and he'd bet she wouldn't let him off easily. In the two conversations they'd had, she'd impressed him as a strong woman, not easily fooled by a silver tongue.

She waved a hand and blew out a breath as if to dismiss the entire incident. "It's okay. Part of your opinion is true."

Thankful he'd been working on his patience, he waited for her to continue, not intending to slip his proverbial foot back into his mouth.

"I can understand why you'd want to check the place out. There's enough talk in the village about the future of Cherry Orchard, but I'm not interested in selling. It means way too much to me, and I promised my grandfather to keep his dream going."

"What was his dream, if you don't mind me asking?"

"Did you notice the view of the bay when you drove up? And the cherry tree line?"

Roman nodded, remembering the view. Impressed didn't cover it. "You bet I did. The property is stunning."

"Our location offers a unique experience for our patrons. It's not so much playing a round of golf on a cute course. It's the sense that you've connected with nature on a whole new level. In a couple of weeks, when the scent of cherry blossoms is in the air and the water warms, it feels as if you've stepped into heaven."

"Sounds magical," Roman added.

"We prefer the word enchanting," she said, a smile curving her lips.

Roman grinned. "I stand corrected." He didn't miss

the light in her eyes. Lexi was passionate about the place and meant what she said. She's not selling.

This wasn't going as he had planned. Adding to the pile with all the others, he might as well let another course that could've worked out fall to the wayside. Later, he'd give his uncle a return call, tell him it was a bust, and get the next assignment. He couldn't waste his precious time. Not with the clock ticking in his head.

"What exactly are you after, Mr. Hart? Is it a golf course or a program for kids? What means more to you?"

Her question intrigued him, taxing him in a way that he wasn't familiar with. He drew in a long breath. "Being on a golf course is like sleeping in a warm bed. It feels like home. I'll probably always dream about owning a course of my own, but my program takes priority. I'd like to have it piloted this summer."

"Why the push?"

"Let's just say I have a good reason." Roman wasn't about to share his timeline with her. He was used to the solitude of living alone and rarely shared private matters with anyone, even his uncle. His life reflected that of a single man, moving from one course to the next.

Roman turned, intending to head toward his truck. He glanced back and said, "I understand. I'll be on my way. Good luck with everything." He wasn't a bully or a shark. He followed his uncle's request and did what he was asked to do. It didn't work out. End of story. He'd simply pick up where he left off—on his way to the next job.

"Wait a minute," Lexi called out after him.

~

Lexi wasn't certain what to make of the man who'd appeared out of nowhere. Well, he wasn't a stranger anymore. She'd met him in the hardware store. The fact was she needed help and he was qualified for the job.

Her mind raced through her options. The course was in disrepair and they needed money to buy out Uncle Bill. Roman was probably good at his job, having spent ten years in the business. And he needed a course to launch his program for kids. She liked the sound of that. She scrutinized the man standing in front of her. Strong shoulders, about six feet in height, well-calloused hands, a handsome face weathered by the sun. He was used to putting in a hard day's work. But would he go for her idea? She'd never know unless she asked.

"How about we help each other out?" She couldn't believe she dared to ask the question. The idea in her head rolled off her lips before she had the chance to change her mind. No one closest to her would say she was spontaneous, but she could've fooled them all right now. The concern about the immediate future of Cherry Orchard overrode her fear of sounding impulsive. She had to fight to make this work and might as well start right now. What's the worst that could happen? He'd say no?

His brows knit together as he eyed her suspiciously.

Lexi couldn't blame him. Maybe she had overreacted earlier in the parking lot, but she'd always been defensive about the golf course. It was her safe place, her little piece of heaven on Earth.

"We need some maintenance work done before we open next month," she began, breaking the awkward silence. "And we could also use some advice on how to…ah, how to…"

Lifting an eyebrow, he asked, "Step into the 21st century?"

She chuckled. He had a pleasant sense of humor, too. Maybe working with him wouldn't be so bad after all. Certainly, watching him put in a hard day's work would be enjoyable. "Yes, something like that. Nothing over the top. The place is dear to my heart, just as it is, but I'll admit it could use some slight improvements."

"What are you proposing?"

"We could offer you a salary, nothing you're used to, I'm sure."

Roman laughed, bringing a smile to Lexi's lips. She liked his quick wit.

"Here's what's in it for you. We have deep roots in our community. We could give you the credibility you need to introduce your program. This is a tight-knit group of people who invest in the small businesses in our county. With some of your marketing expertise, we could attract the big decision-makers and those interested in sponsoring your program to the course."

He raced a hand through his dark hair, revealing the curls at the nape of his neck. She was noticing more about this man by the minute.

Lexi breathed a small sigh of relief. She could see his growing interest reflected in his eyes. *He's considering it! Good.* This was crazy and so unlike her, but they were in a bind. Maybe it was impulsive and not well thought out but her skill set for running a business was subpar. "Why don't you sleep on it and we can talk in the morning?"

He gave her a quick smile. "Thank you, Lexi."

What is he thanking me for? Now she was confused. "For what?"

"Surprising me."

Chapter 4

Lexi stewed over the situation with Roman on the drive to Cherry Orchard the next morning. The wait was excruciating. She needed his help, and he needed a venue to pilot his program. Tapping the steering wheel with her fingertips, she waited for the traffic light to turn green.

Even if Roman accepted the position, the problem of generating extra revenue to purchase Uncle Bill's shares remained, but God probably had better things to do than focus on all of her life's challenges. "I'll try not to keep You too busy, Lord, but we both know I'm not ready for this task and I may never be." Lexi whisked off her prayer and stepped on the gas when the light flickered over.

Pulling into the golf course, she drove her vehicle to the back employee lot. The crew would be in, probably enjoying a second cup of coffee. She'd scheduled a nine o'clock morning meeting to kick off the start of the new season. This would be the first time she'd walk in her grandfather's shoes as their supervisor and those shoes weren't quite comfortable yet.

She pulled open the steel door and stepped inside. "Good morning, everyone."

Everyone seemed to lower their coffee cups at once and then said, "Morning, Boss."

Although she was a floor manager at the hardware store, this new title from the crew would take some getting used to. She'd supervised employees before, many of them, but working at the hardware store didn't have quite the same meaning as it did here at the golf course. She was personally invested here and prayed she had the wherewithal to make it a premier course once again.

"Just a reminder we have our first annual meeting to kick off the new season in about thirty minutes at the clubhouse," Lexi announced to almost a dozen employees. She saw their heads nod and heard the mm-hmms. But it was the uncertainty in their eyes that made a powerful impression on her. The immediate weight of responsibility as the new owner and their boss hit her hard. They were relying on her for their jobs. She wouldn't let them down, or her sisters, or Nana. She had every intention of lifting the course out of the red and turning a profit again. "Good to see all of you this morning. I'm looking forward to our meeting at nine." She hoped she had on her most confident smile."

Lexi glanced at her phone and hustled toward the clubhouse. There was still plenty of time to talk with Roman before the meeting. Her heart thumped with anticipation, hoping he arrived early. He didn't strike her as someone who wasted time, and she expected his decision first thing this morning.

To her happy surprise, Lexi found him driving the last screw into the hinge of the exterior door to the clubhouse. He was taking it upon himself to finish one of the tasks on her list. With so much to do yesterday, she'd completely forgotten about the loose hinge. She grinned. "I take it this means you've made your decision to accept the job?" she asked, hoping she was right in her assumption.

Roman swung his gaze to face her head on. Eyes bright, cheeks flushed, and his smile intact, the man appeared to be ready to climb Mount Everest. His take-charge demeanor had a way of turning her eye. After laying his hammer down, he nodded. "You've got yourself a maintenance man and a consultant on an as-needed basis."

Lexi sighed with relief. This is what she was hoping for. Now she could breathe easier. She'd tackled the first hurdle. "Terrific. Welcome aboard, Mr. Hart." Lexi offered her hand, which fit easily into his. His handshake was firm. Did he pull her toward him ever so slightly? The scent of musk and leather bombarded her senses, in a good way.

"I hope this means you'll begin calling me Roman."

Lexi nodded. "Of course. And, please, do the same."

"Maybe you should clarify the same? Should I call you Lexi? Or is it Lex? Or perhaps Alexandra?"

Lexi raised her eyebrows. *He's toying with me.* "Lexi will do just fine, Mr. Hart…I mean Roman."

Roman rubbed his palms together. "Excellent. We're off to a running start."

"What's all the commotion about?" Ellie stepped onto the deck with Analise two steps behind her younger sister. Both sisters convinced Lexi that they wanted to be present for the first meeting of the year. It was a big day.

Lexi turned to her new hire. "Roman Hart, meet my sisters and co-owners of the golf course, Analise and Ellie Russo. Analise is handling the legal side of things for us, and Ellie is an interior decorator with a firm here in the county. Roman is the contractor I told you about who can handle the renovations and consulting if needed."

"Ladies, it's a pleasure." Roman directed his attention first to Analise. "I can imagine what an asset you are as legal counsel. Lawyer?" he asked, as he shook her hand.

"Third-year law student at Marquette." Analise's smile reflected her accomplishments in a brutal curriculum.

Lexi's heart swelled with pride at all her older sister had managed, despite the major loss of their patriarch.

"Graduation in your sights?" Roman asked.

"You bet it is," Analise said. Her smile widened and her eyes held hope for the future that a hard-earned education would bring.

"Good for you." He turned to the youngest of the three. "Ellie, it's a pleasure."

Ellie shook Roman's hand. "If you need ideas to spruce up the clubhouse, I'm more than happy to help out. I didn't get far from sharing my ideas with our grandfather."

Roman smiled. "I know how that feels."

"Roman, I filled my sisters in on our conversation yesterday. They're on board with our agreement," Lexi said.

Ellie's face softened. "Your program for kids sounds very admirable. A former client of mine is the superintendent of schools. Would a meeting with him help you out?"

Roman's eyes widened. "It absolutely would."

Analise turned toward Lexi. "Did you tell Roman about the guest cottage?"

"Oh, no. I completely forgot," Lexi said. "We have a small cottage on the property. It was one of the first structures built after our grandfather purchased the land and overlooks the first few holes on the course. If you haven't made accommodations in the village yet, you're more than welcome to use it. It's not large, but it is adequate—nice bed, small eat-in kitchen, TV, and a fireplace. It comes along with the salary."

Roman paused as he considered the offer. "That would certainly help me out. I like the idea. It'll allow me to live and breathe the course. Get a good feel for it."

"I've stayed at the cottage from time to time, especially when I have something on my mind," Lexi said.

Ellie huffed. "I'm surprised you haven't moved in permanently."

"And I just might do that one day," Lexi teased. It was one of her favorite places to be. Sitting on the porch in one of the wooden chairs, watching the sunrise with a cup of coffee, brought her immense comfort to her. She rubbed her hands together. "Why don't we go inside and get started?"

Lexi led the way, and the group followed her inside. She turned to Roman. "We have our first staff meeting for the season set for nine o'clock. Are you comfortable addressing the group after I introduce you?"

"Let's do it," he said.

His enthusiasm had rubbed off on her. The jitters

she'd felt earlier while addressing the staff seemed to disappear, at least for now. Would she ever feel confident enough to take the helm of this business? She'd been groomed to do so, yet something so deep inside of her caused an angst she couldn't identify much less get rid of. What was it?

~

Roman followed Lexi and her sisters to the small dining area inside the clubhouse. Since arriving in Door County, his system of approaching new jobs was out the window. Last night, he'd explained to his uncle Lexi's job offer, but oddly, no sound advice came from him. Usually, his uncle was full of opinions and advice. Had the well of wisdom gone dry? The counsel he did offer was to sleep on it, exactly what Lexi had suggested he do. So, that's what Roman did.

After waking early this morning, he'd stopped in at the Perfect Cup Café. Over a cup of Door County cherry coffee and an iced scone, his mind drifted as he considered his options. Keeping what was most important at the forefront of his mind...the program...the decision came quickly. When he recognized the great opportunity that was right in front of him, he quickly finished his breakfast, drank his coffee, and drove to Cherry Orchard. One day he'd own a place he could call his, but the time wasn't now. The program took priority.

Now that he'd accepted the position, Roman scanned the clubhouse interior while Lexi prepared for the meeting. He watched her move about the room like a little worker bee, shuffling papers and straightening tables and chairs. He spotted her nervous energy and wondered about the source. Time would fill in the details, as it always did for him. Another lesson in patience was headed in his direction.

Roman's gaze drifted across the room as he absorbed the details. As he surveyed his surroundings, he made a mental inventory of what had to go and what could stay. Less than a dozen unmatched sets of tables and chairs were scattered about in no particular order. There was a modest bar area with an electric grill in the corner, which probably offered hot dogs and sausages during the season, but was both unimpressive and uninviting.

Worn carpet patterns on the major walkways were hard not to notice. It was easy to deduce that business had been good here once upon a time, but it was time for change. *Hmm.* There were no big screen TVs or a jukebox. The thriving clubs he knew found ways of attracting players to food and drink after they played golf. He was happy to see the oversized windows which offered a view of the Bay and the first tee box, but they needed replacement. Special seating would be nice, inviting patrons to linger and stay a while.

He pictured Lexi's description of the budding trees and warm sun and how stunning it would be in only a few weeks. They had to take advantage of that view, which meant the cloudy windows had to go.

When the staff walked in and took their seats, Roman joined Lexi at the front of the room. After announcements, old business, and the election of officers, she introduced him to the group. This was the part he never enjoyed, breaking the ice. From experience, he worked off the assumption that the staff viewed him as an intruder who would take apart their beloved establishment brick by brick. He'd tackle that fallacy head-on.

"First off, I want to assure all of you that my initial role is that of an observer. Everyone should continue performing their jobs. I'm here to help turn things around. I'd like to…" Before Roman could articulate the rest of his sentence, Lexi interrupted him.

"Mick, please stay," she said. Turning to Roman, she placed a hand on his arm. "I'm sorry for interrupting, Roman."

Roman jerked his head to follow Lexi's gaze to an employee who was striding toward the exit. When Mick paused and turned to answer Lexi, Roman spotted the country club's logo on his cap. He was a loyal employee.

"Don't like change. Never did," Mick spat, "and neither did Mr. Russo."

Lexi gazed up at him with doe-like eyes. *She's not sure what to do.* Remembering a brief conversation, he'd had with her, Roman recalled it was Mick's responsibility to get golfers signed in for play. He placed the man to be in his late fifties. As the eldest in attendance today, Roman feared a mutiny among the group if Mick left the room. He'd seen that happen before. He had to think of something fast to gain this man's trust.

"Mick, what would you say if we added a starter booth for you? A place where you'd have a ledger of reservations for the day right in front of you, a supply of scorecards and pencils, and a way to communicate with the front office?"

Mick's eyes widened, but he was quick with a response to Roman's suggestion. "The regulars already know to come up to the bar to check in."

"We could change that. Have them check in right

away with you. There'd be a period of transition for them, but I think you'll love having better control over your players."

Roman knew he found what was important to Mick when the employee shrugged. "Might work," he said.

"And how about we get you some help for course control? An ambassador or two. Maybe a couple of teenagers looking for a summer job."

The older man's eyes widened. "I'd like that. I always felt I had two jobs, and it's awfully hard to keep play moving out there when you're checking in players."

Mick returned to his seat and both men nodded at each other as if silently making a gentleman's agreement. He'd stick around at least for the time being. Roman turned to Lexi and gave her a reassuring smile.

"Thank you, Mick. This is a good example of the input I'll be looking for from everyone," Roman said. After recognizing Mick's frustration, he expected more challenges would surface down the road. If he could help fix this problem, he'd be well on his way to getting cooperation from everyone else in the room.

Roman opened the floor to questions rather than an itinerary of what he planned to do and when. He answered them individually and informed them about his experience, his expertise, and the consulting side of his business. He explained how he'd installed new clubhouse siding, replaced roofs and faulty irrigation systems, installed new windows, and redefined course layouts, including brand-new greens. His experience spanned from working with heavy equipment to negotiating prices and hiring subcontractors when needed.

After satisfying everyone in the room, Roman

shared the significance of their input in developing a game plan for each department. After the team left, he turned to Lexi. "Ready to show me the course?"

She stared at him with a blank look on her face. Usually always in control, he found her hesitation interesting.

"Are you sure?" she asked.

Roman grinned.

Chapter 5

Lexi gazed out from the club's dining room windows at the gray sky. She hoped Roman would do the same and change his mind about touring the golf course. The sun had disappeared, hiding behind thick cumulus clouds, and the biting spring wind left the tree limbs bending in protest. She shivered just thinking about climbing into her golf cart. As much as she loved winter, she hated to be cold, despite her Wisconsin roots. "The warmest part of the day is long past, and it's a little brisk out there for a tour."

Roman shot a glance outside then turned to her. "The season opener is coming up. I'd like to see it now."

Lexi picked up on the immediacy in his voice. She pushed her opposition to the side. If he wanted to see the course, she'd show him the course.

"Okay. I'll get the cart and pull up by the curb." As Lexi strode toward the cart corral, she motioned for her sisters to join her. She wanted to say goodbye to them before they left. They enjoyed a special birthday weekend together, but she knew Analise was anxious to head back to school, and Ellie mentioned a stop at the studio that she had to make.

Ellie hustled up to Lexi's side and gave her sister a soft elbow jab. "I can see what's happening here."

Lexi gazed back at her sister with wide eyes, surprised she'd noticed Roman's expertise with the group. "You noticed too? I thought Roman handled his part of the meeting beautifully. By asking the staff for their opinions, he's pulling us all together. We have a lot to get done. It was a smart move on his part."

Ellie waved away Lexi's comment. "I didn't mean that. I'm talking about the slow burn between you and our hero."

Analise joined them. "Here we go. Miss Matchmaker is at it again. She did the same thing to me when I told her about my study partner, Nathan."

Lexi gave her older sister a questioning glance. "But you're dating him now, aren't you?"

Analise shook her head, trying her best to diffuse Lexi's point. "That's not the point."

Lexi knew better. She and Nathan had been dating for almost six months now. She chuckled. "It isn't?" she asked, drawing out her question.

Analise brushed Lexi's comment aside.

Ellie beamed, interrupting the two. "I have a sixth sense about these things. You'll see."

Lexi raised her hands, trying to stop further discussion. "He simply asked me for a tour of the course. There's not much to make of that."

"Well, he's tall, dark, and definitely handsome, and the way he looks at you. Ooh-la-la. I can see what's coming between you."

Lexi wanted to groan, hearing the swoon in Ellie's

voice. "Oh, Ellie. There's too much going on here to get starry-eyed now." Lexi turned to Analise. "I suppose you're heading back?"

Analise nodded. "I have to. Classes resume tomorrow but keep me in the loop. This is going to be exciting with Mr. Hart on our team."

"Don't worry. I'll keep a watchful eye on them." Ellie winked.

Lexi rolled her eyes at Analise, ignoring her younger sister's comment. Despite Roman's good looks, with the task list ahead of them, romance was the furthest notion in her mind. "Drive safe, sis," she said.

"I'll be back for opening weekend." Analise gave Lexi a warm hug and whispered in her ear. "You can do this, Lex. Gramps chose you as operations manager for a reason. You need to push aside your doubts about yourself and believe."

Lexi's back stiffened. "Believe? In what?" She softened when she recognized their mother's smile on Analise's face.

"Not in what," Analise said, "but in you. Let go of all those self-doubts you seem to have about yourself."

"You make it sound so easy. Always their father's favorite, Analise couldn't control the attention their father lavished on her as much as Lexi strived to receive it. "I'm sorry, Lise."

Analise managed a smile. "It's okay. The point is, we all believe in you, including Gramps so now it's time to get busy."

Lexi nodded grateful for her sister's forgiveness and what she said about Gramps. He did believe in her. When was she going to follow his lead? She waved a last goodbye when Analise was about to leave. Resuming her stride toward the golf cart corral, she turned to Ellie. "If you have time, could you rough out some ideas to liven up the clubhouse? Oh, and keep the changes to a minimum. We're on a tight budget."

Ellie nodded. "I'd love to. I'll take down some dimensions before I head out. I might even have some leftover fabric from another job we can use to curb costs. Call if you need anything else. And Lex?"

"Hmm?" Lexi zipped up her jacket and then reached for one of the golf cart keys hanging on the rack.

"Keep an open mind moving forward. You've been so preoccupied at work you haven't given love a chance."

Lexi gave Ellie her big-sister glare. "Just because I'm not a fan of dating apps doesn't mean I'm closed off to dating completely."

Ellie shrugged. "It works for some, but not for others. I guess I'm one of the lucky ones. But Lex, maybe someone's looking out for you and delivered a handsome, eligible bachelor on your doorstep for a reason."

"How do you know he's even available?" Lexi asked. She didn't want to stir this pot of romantic ingredients in her sister's head yet, wondering if Ellie knew more about their new hire than she did.

"No ring and no mention," Ellie giggled. "I know the signs."

"Well, I'm glad you're looking out for me," Lexi teased and hugged Ellie.

"Someone has to! See you later."

Lexi supposed Ellie had a point. Instead of focusing her attention on dating, she'd devoted all of her energy to her job, but it paid off. She realized her goal and made it to upper management at the hardware store with a set of transferable skills she could use at the golf course. Yet, her hesitation with the idea of taking over frightened her silly. *Why?*

Without more time to ponder her dilemma, Lexi pulled up alongside the curb, waiting for Roman. She spotted him through the windows, patting Mick on the back. *Wow!* What a turnaround. She watched as Roman bent his head, listening intently to what Mick was saying. He held one hand on Mick's back, the other in a firm handshake.

Lexi studied the men. If Roman steered Mick any farther from the window, she'd lose sight of him. *Stop moving!* She leaned in closer, pressing against the steering wheel. When she shifted her weight, her foot inadvertently landed on the horn button, strategically placed on the floorboard.

Honk!

Lexi gasped as she pulled her foot from the foghorn alert. She might as well have rung a bell to get his attention.

To her horror, Roman whirled around and grinned. She sat back in her seat, trying to disappear into the cushion. He gave her a thumbs up.

Great going, girl. Now he knows you were watching him.

It wasn't long before Roman slipped into his jacket and made his way across the deck. For the first time since she'd met him, Lexi noticed the limp. *Why hadn't I noticed that before?* She wondered what had happened. Once he was inside the cart, Lexi motioned to her side. "You may want to zip up the enclosure."

The color of richly browned oak leaves with specks

of amber came to mind when his eyes met hers. Fluttering warmth swirled inside of her. Roman Hart was a handsome man. He turned his broad shoulders and made quick work of the job, zipping up the plastic window.

With his back to her, Lexi noticed the dark curls at the nape of his neck, slipping beneath his jacket collar. She forced her eyes back on the golf cart path. Ellie's silly suggestion must've wiggled itself into her brain. Doing her best to regain her composure, she hit the gas with too much gusto, throwing Roman backward into his seat with a hard *thump*. "Sorry," she said with an apologetic smile.

Roman chuckled, revealing a good sense of humor. She liked that in a man. "You don't have to apologize for being excited to get started. It's a good sign."

She breezed past the parking lot and toward the first tee. The drive was already clearing her head and chilling the heat in her flushed cheeks.

"I can see why you call it an enchanting experience," Roman commented.

"Right!" She was hoping the cherry tree line would impress him. "It's one of the few courses that offers close access to a live cherry orchard. It's not uncommon for players to stop along the way and pluck a few cherries from the trees while they're playing." She hoped to impress him with this special feature of the course. Lexi imagined the wheels turning in Roman's head.

"Hmm. Does that cause a back-up for play?" Roman pulled out his notepad and made a note.

Lexi fumed. *Does he want to eliminate that too?* Although, his question surprised her, she hoped Roman didn't want to change everything about their club but isn't that what golf consultants did? Get rid of the obsolete and usher in the new. "I suppose it could. We never really paid attention. It was more important for players to enjoy their surroundings than the pace of play."

"The added staff for Mick will help to remedy that if we find that's a problem."

Lexi raised an eyebrow. Had she said it was a problem? She didn't appreciate his tone, yet was curious about the notes he was writing down in that little book of his. Leaning toward him, she tried sneaking a peek at the pad. "Hmm, keeping notes now?"

"Just want to have all the facts straight," he flipped the tablet closed, returning it to his back pocket.

Lexi returned her attention to the path and the first tee box. It was important to her that he understood why the course was unique and not just another project for him. She started with the rocky coastline juxtaposed against the serene view of the course, the winding path and foliage that would soon fill in, and the ability to view Eagle Bluff Lighthouse up ahead.

"My grandfather wanted the course to be more than golf but an experience you can only find here. The bridge is a good example of his wish." She lowered her speed as they drove over the worn timber logs that sagged from the weight of the cart.

Roman peered out the plastic window and then back at her. A look of bewilderment moved over the chiseled features of his face. "But there's no water. Why a bridge?"

Lexi laughed as she stepped on the gas with less force this time. Roman was a practical man with a discerning eye for what should stay and what was unnecessary. But in contrast, he was clueless about the emotional connection her grandfather had for the course.

"You're right about that, but I want you to imagine that you're on a journey. One you've never been on before. Yes, you're here to play eighteen holes of golf, but you begin to realize you're in for a lot more ... a connection with nature with some of the best scenery in Door County."

Again, he reached for his notepad and scribbled something down. *Geez!*

Edging closer to him, Lexi eyed his notebook. She was almost able to make out the first word. She wiggled a little closer. Then she remembered—the pothole! Her heart raced as she pulled a hard left and missed the crater by mere inches. She slammed on the brakes but not fast enough. They ended up buried in the thicket and colliding with each other on the bench seat. Roman's notebook lay on the floorboard. His pencil rolled to a stop by one of his shoes. He placed his hands on top of hers on the wheel. Warmth radiated up her arms. Lexi's heart sped up. It felt wonderful.

Hands still pressed lightly on hers, he turned to her with a wide grin.

Now her insides were bubbling over, leaving her speechless—utterly, miserably, remarkably tongue-tied.

"If you want to know what I'm jotting down, please just ask. Otherwise, I'm going to suggest you get seatbelts installed." He chuckled after making his point.

Lexi slipped her hands from their hiding place under his and placed them on her chest. Thank goodness he had a sense of humor. "You're right. Sorry about that. Shall we continue?"

Roman picked up his writing materials and tucked

them away. He unzipped his side of the canvas enclosure, jumped out of the cart, and then positioned his body against the front end of the machine, revealing strong biceps. "Back her out nice and slow."

Lexi wasn't certain it was necessary, but she sure enjoyed watching Roman manhandle the cart. Once out of the ditch and Roman back in the vehicle, Lexi pulled up to the first tee box. *Welcome to one of the best days of your life.* She must've read that sign a million times and still loved it. She had no idea how Roman would react. This would be interesting.

Roman craned his neck to get a full view. "Now that's something."

Lexi beamed. She was proud of what her grandfather had built. So much of his heart and soul remained right here on this course. "This is just the start. All the odd holes have something unique about them."

"Why just the odd holes?"

Lexi smiled, recalling her grandfather's rationale on the topic. "Gramps believed odd numbers got a bad rap in life, so he made them special here."

When Roman chuckled, Lexi realized she was having a good time. Where had that sour attitude come from earlier? Now, she was glad they'd taken the tour. They'd reached the halfway point with a stunning view of the Bay. Roman pointed to a bench that was perched on a small hill. "Is that your property up there too?"

"It is. Would you like to see it?" Her heart thundered in her ears. She'd love to show Roman the most memorable spot on the course with a stunning view of the lighthouse on a clear day. Plenty of engagements happened on that hill.

He nodded and Lexi headed up the embankment.

"It's called Lookout Point."

Lexi slowed when they reached the white-washed concrete bench so Roman could read the insignia, *For Saying Yes.* What would a man like Roman think of such an endearment? He was a wanderer. A man without roots. It wouldn't surprise her if he couldn't relate at all to her grandfather's romanticism.

After she parked, they followed a grass path to the view that waited for them at the hilltop. Lexi gazed into the expansive Bay waters, listening to the waves crash against the shoreline and refueling her soul while she gave Roman all the time he needed.

"Let me guess. Was that your grandfather's proposal back there on the bench?"

"It is. That was the kind of man he was. He always told us he'd loved our grandmother since the second grade."

Roman's jaw dropped. "That's amazing."

Almost on cue, the evening's sunset was ready to put on a show. The last burst of yellows, oranges, and a hint of purple seeped into the horizon. Twilight, Lexi's favorite time, was near, and the wind they'd been avoiding all day had mellowed to a breeze. Lexi inhaled as much of the sweet Bay water air as her lungs could hold. Peace as sweet as the scent of cherry blossoms filled her. Maybe her concerns about Roman were unfounded and this arrangement was going to work out after all. She hoped so. She needed it to work.

Roman placed his hands on his hips, gazing at the view. "Stunning. Do you know how lucky you are to have this every day of your life?"

Lexi swooned inside. He was beginning to understand. "I do, and that's one reason I've dedicated my life to this course. It's like no other in the area. It's special."

They watched the boats travel up the eastern coastline for a while. Each enjoying the moment in their own private way. The small vessels navigated the choppy waters just as she was trying to navigate the changes in her world.

After watching the last rays melt away, Lexi's thoughts drifted back to the man standing next to her. Stopping at the most revered spot among the Russo family with him was a wise move. Now he would finally understand what made Cherry Orchard unique. It was important to her that this wasn't just another project along the line for him. She wanted, no, she *needed*, him to care, even to a small degree.

With his gaze fixed ahead and a look of serenity on his handsome face, he popped a handful of chocolate candies into his mouth and offered some to her. He was certainly at ease. "So, why isn't this spot included as part of the course?" He asked in between chomping on the sweets. "It's incredible. We could easily add…"

"Absolutely not." Lexi heard the snap in her voice. She shot Roman a daggered look. A bitter disappointment chased away every piece of calm that had filled her only a moment ago. She foolishly assumed he was on the same page, especially after sharing Lookout Point with him. "This is where my grandfather proposed. It's where their legacy began. Your suggestion of adding it to the course would destroy its meaning. Some things are sacred, Roman, and this is one of them." She stomped back to the cart.

Roman crossed his arms. "Of course. It's just…well, never mind, it's not important now, if that's how you feel. I'll try to be more understanding."

"I hope you so," Lexi said, but her doubts about Roman were mounting. He didn't even come close to understanding what the golf course meant to her and her family. Lexi knew without that insight, there was a potential for recklessness in his decision-making. She didn't want to be constantly at odds with this man and understood change was needed, but some things, like Lookout Point, were non-negotiables.

"Let's move the whole idea to the back burner for now," he suggested.

Lexi remained silent hoping he understood that as an absolute. She returned to her seat. How was she to proceed without stirring up her anger all over again? Would Roman want to change everything about the club? He had a long way to go before he understood what it meant to her. Without that understanding…Lexi shook her head.

"We'll get this place turned around. That's what's most important," he said and climbed in next to her in the cart.

She heard the reassuring tone in his voice, yet it brought no comfort. "You're right back on the same track, aren't you? Cherry Orchard needs tender loving care. It doesn't need to be turned around. It's a one-of-a-kind course, including all of its special landmarks. Why can't you understand that?"

Roman was quick to raise defensive hands. "I get you don't want to make any changes as far as Lookout Point is concerned, but I need you to work with me on some of the other ideas I'd like to implement."

Lexi nodded. "I'll try, Roman." But she was growing concerned about whether they could work together and find a middle ground. If his suggestion for Lookout Point was an example of his ideas, they were oceans apart.

"Do we agree that we need to get people back and playing on the course again?"

"Yes. Totally," she said. There was no arguing that point. Players meant revenue, and revenue meant the ability to buy Uncle Bill's shares.

"We'll get through this together, Lexi."

As they drove back to the clubhouse in the peacefulness of the early evening, Lexi grew quiet, doing her best to calm her frayed nerves. His ability to get her riled up was a concern. She questioned if every change he wanted to make would end up in an argument. She took a chance to hire him. *Did I make a mistake?* Even if she had, it was too late now.

They'd signed a contract.

Chapter 6

Concerned with the quarrel between them over Lookout Point, Roman realized he'd eliminated a big distraction for Lexi with his notepad tucked away. Her attentiveness to the path had improved significantly. She drove the golf cart back to the clubhouse without a mishap. Eventually, their easy conversation resumed. He wasn't surprised that Lexi knew every landmark, pointing out unique details along the way. The tenderness in her voice when she talked about the course's attractions was a complete clash from the hot temper woman a moment ago.

Why was the woman so hard-headed? Roman wasn't sure he'd met anyone so stubborn and so single-focused. Always up for the challenge, Roman chuckled to himself. The Lord had certainly given him a handful this time around. He needed to find a fresh approach. With plenty of suggestions scrawled out on the pages of his notepad, he'd figured out that he better come up with a new way of communicating with her and fast. Being at opposite ends of an argument would place them in a stalemate position, a place he didn't want to be.

This situation with Lexi baffled him. He was usually good at finding common ground with people. A trait he'd picked up along the way in the consulting side of his business. *What's the problem here?* He thought about the woman sitting next to him. What matters to her? What makes her tick? Relentless, firm, and unyielding were all words that quickly came to mind, het, there was a tenderness in her eyes and her voice whenever she spoke of Cherry Orchard. Her roots ran deep, and he'd better consider that from now on. This job would not be like the others.

As she drove, Roman made it a point to pay more attention as Lexi filled him in on the small nuances he never would have noticed...a bend in the road leading to a fork in the path, a boulder to avoid, or a low tree limb where many players stopped for picture taking. She described the special touches she hoped to add, the one-of-a-kind view they presented, and the unique experience she wanted the players to walk away with when they finished their rounds. He picked up on the softness in her voice. She really loves the place. Roman rubbed his jaw. Maybe I could meet her halfway to reach a common ground with her.

Roman grimaced as he rarely allowed himself that deep of a connection ... to *feel* something. Usually, he distanced himself from forming a personal bond. People could get hurt if they got too close to him. His injury was a reminder of that truth and the cool relationship he now had with his parents. Keeping people at arm's length had worked for Roman, but if he wanted to turn this club around, implement the changes he knew had to take place, and work side-by-side with Lexi, he'd have to allow himself to care. And he'd better start right now, but he needed to be careful. Lexi Russo was the last person he wanted to hurt.

Leaning in her direction, Roman said, "Lexi, when I said I'd take the job, that meant I'm one hundred percent committed here. You can trust me, even though I have a feeling I might have to prove that to you."

If he hadn't been watching her, he would have missed the sigh that escaped Lexi's lips. Disappointed, his ribs grew tight. He thought she'd appreciate hearing his intentions, yet it was obvious something still bothered her. Lexi Russo was more complicated than she let on.

She gave him a leveled gaze. "*I'm* responsible for making sure Cherry Orchard stays afloat. My sisters and Nana are counting on me. So are the employees who need their jobs. The community wants to hold on to the landmark, and my grandfather's legacy needs to be handed down to the next generation."

Her lone-wolf approach to problems sounded all too familiar but did he also hear a bit of fear in her words? He certainly could relate to the pressure. He gathered his thoughts and said, "You're right, but I hope you view me as your partner in all of this. You can count on me. And you're not alone here. You've got me now. Why don't we take one step at a time? Let's make that our motto."

Lexi lifted her shoulders, but Roman caught the smile on her lips. "I'll try. But honestly, I'm not used to letting others help."

"Why is that?" Roman was perplexed. Lexi was a captivating, beautiful, and intelligent woman. She must've managed a crew of employees at the hardware store. Why now, is she having trouble delegating?

"I learned the hard way that most people will let you down ... important people. And that changes you. You learn to depend on yourself because it's the safest route to the end. There are no surprises along the way but it's also unsettling, especially with new projects and new responsibilities. I've been comfortable at the hardware store."

Roman nodded, but not before he caught her gripping the wheel a little tighter. Someone in her past had hurt her. Bad. And that hurt still affected her.

When his dad had told him to pack up his gear and move out after the accident, that had cut deep within him in a similar way. But he'd deserved it. His instincts told him Lexi had not. Maybe it wasn't just the course that needed his help, and he was led to Cherry Orchard for more than one reason. He hoped God had picked the right man for the job.

Lexi gave Roman a nervous smile. "I'm sorry. This is very unlike me to open up to someone so easily. You must have a special gift. What is it about you Roman Hart?"

"Oh, I doubt that. I'm an ordinary guy." Roman chuckled. "I'd like to thank you for the enjoyable tour."

"You're welcome. I have to admit, I'd never heard of a golf course consultant until you showed up. How did you end up in this line of work?" She flipped on the headlights and cruised easily through the last couple of holes on the course.

"Well, I guess you could say I fell into it." He realized he had given her a vague response, but Roman normally avoided sharing his personal life with anyone. It wasn't pretty, and if questions arose and dug deep enough, there was little to be proud of. Trouble followed some people, and Roman had learned the hard way that he was one of them. All he had to do was remember how he'd ruined so many lives.

"I'm beginning to understand the need for someone in your capacity."

"I don't make too much of it. In the end, it's mostly maintenance work." Roman preferred to be understood as the average man he was. He was comfortable with his life. He loved his work, had a plan, and leaned on God for understanding.

"Hmm. If you don't mind me asking, how did you end up on the consulting side of your business?"

"Long story." He couldn't blame her curiosity. He blew out a breath knowing it would be hard to relive that moment that had changed his life forever. He considered withholding the truth but was quickly reminded that if he wanted to help others, he had to use his own life experiences to do it. Honesty, like patience, was a virtue he was always working on.

"Ten years ago, right before I left for college ... my life took a detour."

Lexi's pretty eyebrows rose. "A detour? You mean like a semester off to backpack across Europe?"

Roman dropped his head. *If only it was that.* "No. I ended up in a car accident on graduation night because I chose to text and drive."

Lexi gasped. "Oh, no." Despite what had been her intention to return to the clubhouse, she pulled the cart over to the side. The coolness of the evening slipped into the cab.

"The worst part of that was my dad was a cop. He came to the high school and lectured us kids on what not to do while you're driving. Texting, of course, was on the top of his list." Roman felt the same old icy grip of dread.

"You heard his message so many times you stopped listening. Tell me what happened, Roman."

"I was clipping along at a good speed. Had my best girl in the passenger seat. The last thing I remember is cranking up the volume of our favorite song."

Lexi said, "Feeling invincible, I'll bet."

Roman wished he could smile, reliving the moment, but the memory caused an ache deep inside of him to his very core. "With my head in the clouds and my eyes on my phone, I didn't see the broken down car that was parked in my lane. I hit the brakes and cranked the wheel. It wasn't enough. The impact clipped the front end. I not only ended up with a pile of pins and metal in my foot, but the worst was that I robbed my girlfriend of a career in ballet that night in one single, stupid decision."

Lexi's hand landed on his arm with her next breath. Roman's shoulders relaxed, as he felt the warmth of her touch.

"Oh, Roman," she murmured. He recognized the ring of disappointment in her voice, so similar to his father's the night of the accident.

Roman looked away. Shame, both old and new, filled him. "Yup."

"Is that when the dream for your program for kids came into focus for you?"

Roman nodded, turning his attention back to Lexi. "The blessing from that horrible night. But I needed start-up money, so I joined my uncle in golf course maintenance work. When I started sharing some of my ideas with the owners of struggling courses, and they helped, I created a niche for myself."

"And the injury to your foot?"

Roman slapped the side of his leg. "Apparently, I need a daily reminder. Even though I can't play the game anymore, there's no better way to start the day than on the course."

Lexi gave him a blank stare. She looked almost starstruck. "Did I say something wrong?" Roman asked.

"No, just an uncanny coincidence. You repeated my grandfather's mantra for life."

"That is uncanny."

"How did your parents handle what happened?"

"Not well. My dad helped me get my athletic scholarship. After they revoked it, he asked me what I planned on doing now with my future."

"Ouch," Lexi said.

"Yup. Hard lesson learned," Roman admitted, "but that's how I ended up working with my uncle."

"And just like that, a decade flies by."

"You can say that again. As long as we're being honest with each other. Now, it's your turn. How are you planning to work two jobs at the same time? It's going to be awfully hard managing the golf course and the hardware store."

"I took a three-month sabbatical from the store. I don't want any distractions because I'd like to make the move permanent. The store is aware of my intentions."

Roman hoped to breathe some hope into the conversation that had turned serious. "I don't see why that can't happen once you change."

"There is a problem. Our majority shareholder would like to sell us his shares. Developers have already approached him. We need to move quickly before he's tempted to sell us out." Lexi pulled back onto the path and resumed their journey back to the clubhouse.

Roman remembered the conversation with his uncle on the topic. "Yes, my uncle may have mentioned it to me. That's a tough spot, but remember we're a team and we'll figure this out."

"Well, then, I hope you're ready for a challenge." Lexi chuckled, and Roman wished they had more of a journey back to the clubhouse. They'd covered some tough ground and handled uncomfortable moments, but Roman had a good feeling about Lexi Russo. He also enjoyed her company—quite a bit. He spotted the twinkling lights inside the clubhouse as they traveled the last trek down the path.

After stopping the cart, Lexi grinned at Roman. "I'll walk with you to the guest cottage and let you get settled in for the night. It's been an interesting day."

"Sounds good." Roman climbed out of the cart and walked to her side. They passed under a short pergola covered in vines. Once through the wooden structure, he tipped his head back and stared at the star-filled night sky. "Would you look at that?"

Tipping back her head, Lexi gazed into the night sky. "Is that … a shooting star?" she asked. "It's been so long since I've seen one of those."

Roman stepped next to her, close enough that their shoulders were touching. "Close your eyes right now and make a wish. Hurry before it's too late."

Lexi threw him a petulant look. "I'm not sweet sixteen anymore, believing wishes come true."

"Come on, do it anyway. What have you got to lose?"

She answered him with a smile. "Oh, all right," she

said and tipped her head back again, but this time she closed her eyes.

Roman didn't want her to stop believing that good things happen. As he waited, he caught the moonlight casting a milky glow across her skin. When she turned to face him, he felt like a younger man who'd fallen in love too quickly. He fought to catch his breath. She couldn't have looked more beautiful if she'd tried.

"I wished for success in our efforts," she said. Her eyes held that little bit of something … hope.

He returned her smile but knew he couldn't match the radiance of hers. "Same wish on this end. I say the odds are in our favor."

"Thanks for that. It's been a long time since I've wished on a star."

"You need to make that a habit."

Lexi shrugged. "Yeah, maybe you're right. It feels pretty good," she said, then led him down the path toward a bend in the road. "The guest cottage is straight ahead. Here's the key. You should be all set from here."

Something roared inside of Roman, having him question what it'd be like to kiss and hold her. Thankfully, his common sense kicked in. He'd ruined too many lives, including his own, to entertain such risky thoughts. And he couldn't trust that he wouldn't do it again to someone else, given half a chance.

"Good night, Lexi," Roman flipped the key end over end in his fingers. Disappointment tugged at the smooth edges of his heart. He turned and walked toward the little cottage, wishing with each step he had a different life than the one he owned.

Chapter 7

Lexi stood on the eighteenth hole and filled the last scorecard holder with a fresh stack of cards. Before turning back to the clubhouse, she smiled into the rising sun, feeling its early morning warmth on her cheeks. "How am I doing, Gramps?"

For the last few weeks, she'd fought her natural tendency to oppose Roman's ideas. Her strategy had paid off. She worked tirelessly by his side, day in and day out, absorbing as much of his expertise as she could. As a result, they addressed the issues together. It was a partnership that had jelled. When Roman began stepping back in the decision-making, he encouraged Lexi to step up. She understood his intentions—to mold her to take the reins of the business. Because of that strategic move, she graduated from managing people to handling administrative tasks with more ease and familiarity each day. He was so much more than just a maintenance man or a consultant. He'd become her mentor as well. Still, the thought of being on her own, without him, frightened her more than death itself.

Walking into the clubhouse, she found Roman seated at a table. His eyes were glued to his notebook as he paged through it. She spotted him often taking notes to remind himself of the next task or an issue he needed to investigate.

Lexi stopped at his table. "You're certainly focused this morning. What are you working on?"

Roman slipped his pen swiftly behind his ear and notebook into his back pocket. "Morning Lex. A couple of new ideas for the maintenance department."

"Perfect. I'm headed down there right now. Would you like to join me?" Lexi had learned that Roman's suggestions were usually spot on. He certainly seemed like a very capable man who didn't shy away from a hard day's work. Just last week, she'd witnessed him working with the grounds crew laying new sod for the greens. He could have easily backed off of that assignment and accepted his realtor's invitation to check out a golf course near Sturgeon Bay, but he declined that invitation and chose to work with the crew instead. She admired him for that decision. She couldn't help but smile. He was keeping his word.

Roman got to his feet and patted his back pocket. "I have quite a few notes here I'd like to share."

Lexi chuckled. "I figured you would, but I think most of us have lost our fear over your notepad, Roman. Let's head down there."

After a quick walk, Lexi led Roman into the building where they found the crew. As she scanned the area, Lexi noted what the men had already accomplished. The lawn equipment had undergone power washing and the shop floor had been swept clean. Even the compressed air hoses were on their hooks. Someone had thoroughly cleaned the exhaust fans of dust and cobwebs. Tools were hanging neatly on the wall above the shop's long workbench. The faint smell of gasoline lingered in the air. Lexi's heart swelled. The place looked great.

"Good morning, everyone. I'm going to start the day with a word from Roman, who has a short work list for you."

Roman scanned the group. "Gentlemen, a few of you came to me with suggestions. It was exactly what I was hoping for. Looking around, I can see you have everything ready. One suggestion I have is to group supplies. For instance, chemicals and flammables in one area. Seeds and fertilizers in another. Let's separate the herbicides and pesticides. And let's get them all neatly labeled so we can all find what we need quickly."

The ground supervisor got to his feet. "We can take care of that," Eduardo said.

"Good. Today, since the weather is cooperating, I'd like you to check the grounds for any winter damage. Take inventory and report back to me what you think needs to be done out there. If you need to get a hold of me, use these." Roman tossed Mick and Eduardo a walkie-talkie.

"A walkie-talkie?" Mick asked. "Why not text? We all have phones."

Roman stiffened. He rubbed the back of his neck.

Remembering how the accident changed so much for him, Lexi's ears perked. How would he handle this uncomfortable situation?

Roman drew in a breath. "I don't text and found that certain areas of the golf course have poor cell phone reception, therefore the walkie-talkies are more reliable. Turn to Channel 4. Push the orange button and relay your message. It's as simple as that."

"Eduardo, I'd like your team to check all the putting greens, drainage ditches, and especially the retaining pond wall. I've toured the course and made a note of the problems. Now, I'd like to hear from your perspective before we get started."

Lexi caught the excited flicker in Eduardo's eyes. Roman was doing it again—empowering the staff to step up. Eduardo signaled a thumbs up to Roman. "If I have trouble, I'll use the walkie-talkie," he said and lifted his new device into the air.

"Good," Roman said. "I'm counting on you."

"If anyone has a question, ask away. Otherwise, let's get busy." Roman stepped from the limelight and walked with Lexi toward the exit door while the crew hustled to their vehicles.

Roman held the door for Lexi. "There is one more item I'd like to discuss with you while we walk back to the clubhouse."

"Okay, shoot," she said and slid past him and through the doorway.

"I'm going to suggest offering leagues and special events."

Lexi shook her head. "Gramps never wanted leagues. Too many headaches."

Roman squared up his shoulders as they continued their trek up the hill at the same pace. "And he was right. They can be. Event markers would have to be set up, scores tallied, and a special reservation system would have to be installed. On the flip side, league play brings in income immediately. The standard practice now is charging upfront for the entire season."

Lexi hadn't thought of that. She'd heard about other courses in the area charging upfront for the entire season, but she never pursued the idea because of Gramp's stubbornness on the issue.

"Maybe it's time to switch things up. It would help make an enormous difference in the books," Roman suggested.

Lexi paused, not wanting to shoot down what could very well be a good idea. She was learning to be more open-minded.

Roman eyed Lexi. "By adding leagues, we're talking about a good amount of revenue in a short amount of time." His eyes grew more intense as he went on. "And by offering to host a spring and fall banquet, you've created a family of players who'll want to come back year after year."

"That will change the quiet culture we have here completely. It used to be one of the few courses where a player can simply show up and we send them out. With the addition of our reservation policy, it makes that more difficult. By adding league play, I'm afraid it could become nearly impossible."

"You're right. I understand there have been quite a few changes in a short amount of time. But don't you think getting ready for a brand-new season is the perfect time to do it?"

Flipping the invisible coin over in her head, Lexi pondered Roman's argument. She was beginning to understand the benefits of his suggestion. "I do like the idea of extra revenue."

Roman rubbed his hands together. "And right now, you need revenue."

Lexi nodded. It was all starting to make sense to her now. "Let's do it. I'll call the newspaper today and take out an ad that we're now offering leagues. In the meantime, let's get ready and the staff trained."

Roman winced. "We'll have to purchase supplies for the events and get the crew on board. We should expect extra prep work on league days."

Lexi laid a light hand on Roman's shoulder. "It's okay. We have a stash fund for that."

"I get excited when things begin to happen."

Roman pulled a chair from a nearby table and offered one to Lexi after they entered the clubhouse. Before sitting down, he added, "By adding leagues and making these simple additions, you'll have solid numbers in black and white to prove a steady income. It might come in handy when you're negotiating with your Uncle Bill. Leagues create hype. Tournaments are another good idea. Especially a fundraiser."

"I understood your logic for leagues and maybe a special event on holidays, but a fundraiser?" Lexi squeaked. "You're killing me here. We can hardly make ends meet now."

Roman chuckled. "Take a breath. I know this is a lot."

Ellie burst through the door like a waterspout on the Bay, unknowingly putting a pause in their conversation. Her arms were overflowing with bolts of fabric and sketch pads.

"This is so exciting! Do you have a minute? Because I need to show you both some of my ideas." The sketchbooks and fabric bolts spilled from her arms onto the table. She hooked her purse around the back of a chair. "You're going to love this," she said, as she quickly tossed her coat onto a nearby chair.

Lexi smiled, admiring Ellie's enthusiasm. It was obvious she'd placed this little side job at the top of her to-do list. Ready for a diversion from her conversation with Roman about leagues and tournaments, Lexi settled in her chair.

"First off," Ellie said, "I think we should replace the ancient curtains with a fixed cornice. We can add a UV blind that will tuck discreetly underneath the board. You can easily draw it down in the afternoons to diffuse the light."

Roman shifted his gaze in Lexi's direction. "Your sister is probably going to give you a hard time on this one. You'd be blocking the view."

"That's right. Patrons enjoy watching players on the first tee and eighteenth putting green." Lexi crossed her arms. Her disagreement was obvious. She wouldn't budge on this one.

"I thought of that and why I chose this type of weave. It allows you to see right through it. Here, I have a sample in my bag."

Over an hour later, Lexi's shoulders hit the back of her chair. She didn't want to make one more decision. "Okay, one more time. Here it goes."

Roman threw her a quick wink, robbing the tenseness from her voice. She gazed at her sister and reconsidered her response, recognizing all the hard work she'd put into her presentation.

"Yes, to removing the old curtains and adding the decorative cornices and blinds. No way to remodeling the ladies' locker room. That has to wait until next year. And yes, to everything else on that list of yours. Thank you, Ellie, for everything you've done."

Roman reached over and rubbed Lexi's shoulders. "Lots of decision-making today. You're doing great."

"It feels like I'm taking the course apart piece by piece," Lexi said.

Ellie raised her eyebrows and Lexi knew exactly what her artistic yet sometimes overimaginative sister was thinking. When Roman touched her shoulders, that was enough to set off wonderful bells in her sister's head. She'd have to set her straight later. She and Roman had worked out their kinks, and now they were more like a team than ever.

Roman rose from his chair, stretching his long legs. "Good work today, Ellie. This is exactly what I was hoping you'd put together."

"Thank you, Roman. I'll have it installed before opening weekend."

Roman glanced at his watch. "I'm going to head out and see how the crew is doing out on the course. I'll talk with you later, Lex. Bye, Ellie."

After he was out of earshot, Lexi leaned across the table. "Don't start."

"Start what?" The look Ellie gave her didn't convey her implication.

"I know what that fairytale mind of yours is thinking and you can stop right now."

"Well, anyone can see the sparks between you two. Even Mick pulled me aside the other day and told me you would make a fine couple one day. Even *he* can see where this is going."

Lexi frowned. "Really? We work well together, that's all it is."

Ellie placed a light hand on Lexi's back. "Don't let what happened with Dad ruin things for you. You've been doing that for years."

Lexi peered back at the sister she'd always regarded as flighty and free-spirited, not a care in the world. Ellie was always the life of any party. But right now, she saw her sister in a new light. A woman with a potent perspective. But was she right?

Have I pushed relationships away?

If Ellie had a point, Lexi had no idea how to fix it.

~

Stepping outside, Roman drew in as much fresh air as his lungs would hold. He shook his head hoping to clear it out of this funk. When he decided to draw closer to Lexi, he didn't count on his feelings to follow. What had he been thinking? Somewhere between selecting grass seed and helping her navigate the accounting software, he'd grown to love spending time with her. *Is this also part of the plan, Lord?*

Roman shook his head, trying to make sense of it all. Was it the nightly walks that pulled him into this uncomfortable place? *Humph.* That was his big idea too. When she asked if he'd like to meet up again the following night, did he hesitate? No. The night after that? Not for a minute. He looked forward to those walks as much as she did. Maybe more. He even caught himself turning down opportunities to check out available golf courses in the area so he wouldn't miss out on them. He's delayed so many appointments with his realtor he was surprised she still bothered contacting him.

Roman rubbed his jaw. He'd best be careful moving forward. Maybe, he should consider reeling back and creating some distance between himself and Lexi. The problem was, whenever he was near her, he felt like a million bucks. She'd become his counterpart, his backboard for ideas, and she'd made those ideas even better with her suggestions. He loved her laugh, loved how her skin looked in the moonlight, loved her touch. *Uh-oh.*

A cold reality seeped into his thoughts, ruining the moment. This couldn't go on any further. The truth was, he lacked the qualities of a good partner. He had proven that to everyone years ago.

Racing a hand through his hair, he picked up his pace toward the maintenance building. Now he was in over his head. He wondered if he'd lured Lexi into the same place. Did she harbor the same feelings for him as he had for her? Roman rubbed his jaw a second time. He'd have to figure out how to fix this and soon. His heart tanked deep in his chest. The last move he wanted to make was to leave a broken heart behind, especially Lexi's.

Chapter 8

Lexi entered the dining area and spotted Ellie securing the last cornice board for the room's windows. What a transformation it made!

"Ellie, this is fantastic. I love the color scheme."

Ellie beamed. "I know the room used to have a comfortable, worn-in feel, but now I would say it's chic and even a bit trendy. Now take a look at this." She drew down the small weaved shade that was tucked discretely behind the cornice. Lexi would never have noticed it until Ellie pointed it out to her.

"This is exactly what I wanted. It cuts the glare without blocking the view." Lexi placed her hand on the delicate weave and smiled. "I can see right through this."

Ellie nodded. "What's your opinion of the new table and chairs I found at the resale shop?"

Lexi slid her hand along the backside of the blue upholstered chairs, then eyed the white round tables. "It's a nice clean look." She scanned the room. "It all blends beautifully." Maybe delegating the less important tasks wouldn't be as hard as she thought. It would certainly free her up for the more important responsibilities.

Ellie beamed. "It opens up the room, giving the illusion of more space, don't you think? Blue and aqua are the colors of the sea, so it's fitting for the clubhouse. It's subtle but brings the outdoors in."

Lexi brought her hands to her face. "It's perfect." She continued her perusal until a pile of boxes piled on tables drew her attention. She walked toward her sister, now descending from the ladder. "What's all this?" She asked pointing toward them. She feared Ellie had overspent on items they really didn't need.

"Another resale purchase. This time, believe it or not, from a small shop that outfits weddings." Ellie opened one box with a razor knife she withdrew from her pocket, pressed the sides back, and carefully lifted out a small electric lamp.

"How adorable!" Lexi breathed a sigh of relief. She'd been wrong in her assumption. Ellie had curbed her spending.

"Right?" Ellie agreed. "I thought we could center them on the tables for a nightclub vibe. Roman suggested we try to keep players in the dining area after their rounds, spending their money on food and drinks."

Lexi nodded. "I like it, but we'll need to enhance our menu a bit. Maybe we can get a couple of air fryers and offer chicken wings."

"Who doesn't love wings, especially after a round of golf? Did you get the call from the farm yet?" Ellie asked.

"The farm?" Roman asked as he walked toward them.

The scent of freshly cut grass trailed behind him. Lexi couldn't help but admire his physical attributes. His skin already taking on a bit of a tan and his muscles flexed and ready to go. Lexi's stomach fluttered.

He looked as if he'd just jumped off one of the mowers and she wouldn't be surprised if he had. Dragging in grass clippings from his boots and smudges of dirt on his face, he must've tackled an outside project.

Lexi knew, by this time, he much preferred spending his time working physically. The extent of his work behind a desk was the pencil tucked behind his ear and a notepad protruding from a back pocket. The walkie-talkie clipped to his belt had become his reliable source of communication with his staff.

But was he ready to hear about the arrangement they'd had with Taylor Farms? There was only one way to find out. She turned toward him. "We use Taylor Farms as our fertilizer supplier. Eduardo told me yesterday it's ready to be picked up."

"How are you involved with the fertilizer pickup? Usually, the supervisor of the maintenance department handles that responsibility. In your case, that would be Eduardo."

Lexi squiggled up her nose. "It's a little more complicated than that. They don't set a fixed price. It takes a little…negotiating."

"You can say that again." Ellie chuckled.

Roman shook his head, clearly confused. "Negotiating? I'm not sure I follow."

"I have an idea," Ellie said. "Why don't you take Roman with you so he can witness this transaction firsthand? He'd certainly walk away with a better understanding of how things are done around here."

Lexi eyed Roman. Was he up for the challenge? She couldn't remember when the tradition of setting the price for fertilizer began, but smiled to herself, remembering it was her grandfather who came up with the unique system. Maybe she should take Roman along.

She turned to Roman. "Would you like to come along?"

Roman unclipped his walkie-talkie from his belt. "Not sure what's going on here, but count me in. Let me radio Eduardo and let him know where I'll be."

After the call, Lexi and Roman jumped into the haul truck with Lexi in the driver's seat. It was a brief ride over to Taylor Farms, and she wanted to find out more about the man sitting next to her. She lowered her speed and asked, "So, where's home, Roman?"

"If I'm honest, I'm on the road too much to plant any roots. I have a post office box back in Bailey's Harbor, where I grew up."

"That's where your parents live?"

"Yup, but they'll be moving to Arizona this fall. We haven't exactly kept in touch since the accident."

Lexi couldn't imagine being that estranged from her family. "Why not?"

Roman shrugged. "Too painful, I guess."

"I can understand the need to spread your wings and find your way, but why the distance with your parents?"

Roman turned his head to face the window. "Never been the same since the accident."

"I'm sorry to hear that. Surely…one day?" There was always hope in reconciliation. At least, that's what Lexi believed. What could cause such a permanent cut from family?

Roman lifted a shoulder. "Maybe."

Lexi picked up on the hurt in Roman's tone. If only there were a soothing balm for his wound. It was so deep and had taken up residence inside his heart for so long. Now she was beginning to understand the long-term consequences of the accident.

Despite all the drama with her father remarrying a younger woman and her mother moving to Costa Rica, she couldn't imagine cutting ties completely. While her heart gave a tug at his situation, it also presented a question. After losing everything he held dear, had he built a wall around his heart? Without realizing it was happening, she'd grown to care for Roman. Now, it was too late. She was in too deep.

She turned her gaze in his direction and found him still staring aimlessly at the moving landscape. "It seems to me like you've become a remarkable man, despite the odds you've had to endure. But every man needs a night out. How about joining the crew and me for our annual bowling night? You haven't had a free night out since you arrived here.

Roman shrugged a shoulder. "Ah, I don't know. I usually work on the program in the evenings."

His resistance didn't surprise Lexi, now that she had a better understanding of his past. "But it's our tradition to kick off the new season every year," Lexi said, using a persuasive tone. Still, Roman held back. *What on earth is he afraid of?*

"We're down a player and could really use you. You'd be going up against me and my teammates."

Finally, he turned from the window. A wide smile plastered on his face. "That sounds like my kind of challenge.

Lexi turned off the main highway. "Good. Then

we'll expect you."

Roman shifted in his seat. "This is a little farther than I thought. I don't want to be gone too long with the guys out on the course."

Lexi chuckled. "You're beginning to sound like a mother hen. Don't worry about them, Roman. They know what to do even if you're not there."

Roman nodded, doing his best to agree with her, but his posture was too erect as if he were on high alert. Lexi couldn't imagine why. Everything back at the golf course was moving along beautifully, and now she had him coming to the party. She felt on top of the world.

Chapter 9

Roman eyed the *Welcome to Taylor Farms* sign from his seat in the truck. He'd planned to check out another course his realtor had found for him, but when Lexi asked if he'd be interested in going along, he postponed the viewing. With a quick turn of the wheel, Lexi backed up the truck like a pro to one of the delivery bays.

Stepping out of the vehicle, she reached for a cardboard box from the back seat. Roman slammed the door after exiting the truck. What did the box contain that had to do with the meeting? Instead of asking a dumb question, he followed Lexi to a side entrance door. If she felt uneasy about the transaction ahead, she certainly concealed it well.

Finally, Roman couldn't help himself. Whatever was in that box had to be important for her to carry it into the meeting. "So, what have you got in your hands?"

Lexi chuckled. "It's eating you up inside, isn't it?" She stepped aside, allowing Roman to open the door to the shop. "Chet Taylor runs this organic produce farm. We've been purchasing fertilizer from him for decades. It's the same blend he uses in his produce gardens. And you're about to see how important what I'm carrying has to do with today's negotiations."

"Hmm." Roman picked up the familiar odor of motor oil and the spring-clean scent of grass when he entered the shop. Equipment littered the expansive space, yet there was an organized order to it all. Shovels were leaning against a corner wall, tools hung from an oversized pegboard, and heavy equipment lined the length of the building. How he'd love to have a place like this one day. The space alone was impressive.

"If this is your fertilizer supplier, I have a few questions for him after seeing so many barren parcels with no grass on the course."

On the other side of the shop, Roman heard the clanging. A man headed in their direction. Wearing a pair of broken-in jeans, tanned boots, and an insulated heavy shirt, he gave Lexi a warm smile. "Lexi Russo, good to see you. Who's your friend?"

"We've hired a consultant to help us with our opening season this year. Chet Taylor meet Roman Hart."

"Good to meet you," Chet said and offered a firm handshake.

Roman nodded. "Same."

"Is your father available?" Lexi asked, then placed the box on a side table and began loosening the sides.

Finally, Roman would see what the big secret was all about.

Chet chuckled as he whisked off a text message on his phone. "Are you kidding? As soon as he heard you were making your annual visit, he told me he didn't need his afternoon catnap today. He's on his way."

"That's adorable," Lexi smiled.

"So, what do we have to work with today?" Chet asked, eyeing the box in Lexi's hands.

Lexi gave Chet a warning look, but Roman spotted the humor in her eyes. "You don't have to concern yourself about that. You know this is between your father and me."

With a look of disappointment on his face, Chet turned his attention to Roman. "So, golf course consultant. Interesting occupation."

Feeling completely at ease, Roman slid his hands into his pockets. "It keeps me busy, but by the looks of this farm, I can assume the same for you. Lexi tells me the fertilizer she's buying from you today will do the job. Can you bring me up to speed on its composition?"

In Roman's eyes, Chet looked like a hardworking man made from the same cloth as his own, and because of his intuition, he trusted this man. It sure looked as if Lexi had a good relationship with him. An uncomfortable thought breezed through Roman's mind. Had they dated? Were they dating now?

Chet returned from the back of the room, carrying a twenty-pound burlap sack in his arms. He dropped it on the floor between them. "I can tell you this, it's one hundred percent organic. Take a look at the label."

"Nitrogen, phosphorus, and potassium. Okay, the basic three." Then the list went on into more than a dozen other smaller ingredients, including calcium, the king of minerals. Now he had Roman's attention.

Chet repositioned the baseball cap on his head. "Familiar with organics?"

"I know Gramps loved it," Lexi added.

Roman winced. He preferred the quick results he got with the industry's standard. "I'm usually not around for the entire season. I prefer the fast-acting fertilizers."

"Sure. I can understand that. You'll get a quick result, but it won't last. If you care about the health of your grass, this product will be better for your soil. It'll feed the micronutrients. Healthy soil grows healthy grass. Save the commercial fertilizer for spot treatments."

"How many applications of your product will we need?"

Chet raised a finger. "One time, either in spring or fall. I'd recommend the spring and take advantage of the rain that's moving in."

"Is this a local product?" Roman asked.

"It's from the chicken farm, right, Chet?" Lexi asked.

Chet nodded. "Yup. Located right outside the village. It can green up the most stubborn of plants and grasses. I use it on my property and it has never disappointed me."

Roman wasn't sure when he stopped listening. It wasn't hard to imagine the stench that would come from using the product. His experience had him fairly knowledgeable on fertilizers, but chicken manure. This was a first. "Chicken manure? Ah…"

"I know what you must be thinking, but give me a minute here. Because of the way it's processed, there's little odor. Apply it at night, either before a good rain or an irrigation, and you'll feel more than satisfied."

Roman shook his head. "Worth a shot."

Chet nodded. "You won't be sorry. All we have to

do now is wait for the pricing to be figured out between Lexi and my dad."

Roman slipped his pencil behind his ear. "I was surprised to learn that Eduardo isn't handling that part of the process. I assumed I'd be in on the price negotiations today." Roman shifted his gaze to Lexi, who simply lifted her shoulders but said nothing to clarify the mystery, leaving Roman without an explanation. He turned back to Chet.

Chet grinned. "Not here. There's a fine art to this process."

Odd, Roman thought.

The rear door opened and an older gentleman walked into the building. "If it isn't our Miss Lexi. I'm happy to see you." Mike Taylor strode toward Lexi with a smile that brightened his face. Roman observed the older man as he walked toward her. His slow gait, weathered face and hands, and a once strong build told him he'd dedicated his life to his work. The same arduous track Lexi was now on.

Lexi beamed a beautiful smile in Mike's direction. "And you as well, Mike."

The older gentleman extended a hand in Roman's direction. "Mike Taylor, pleasure to meet you."

"Roman Hart, sir. I'm working with Lexi on getting the course ready for the season and making some needed renovations on the course and in the clubhouse."

"He's a golf course consultant," Lexi added.

"Good man. She needs all the help she can get to keep those greedy developers from tearing down the place."

"So, you've heard the rumors too?" Lexi asked.

Mike nodded. "Hard not to. People talk. Glad you're

on board, Roman. I'm sure you'll help make a difference."

"Thank you. I'm glad to be here." Roman couldn't remember fitting in with a community of people as easily as he had here, Chet and Mike now included.

"Are you ready to do this?" Mike rubbed his thick hands together, worn from a lifetime of work. His eyes fixed on the box Lexi had brought.

Lexi wiggled off the cover. "It's your favorite," she said, in a buttery tone, "so I expect a reasonable price."

"You've got to be kidding me," Mike exclaimed. "Is this what I think it is?"

Roman inched forward, more curious about the contents of the box, yet still clueless. This was the oddest price negotiation he'd ever witnessed.

Chet gave him a nudge. "Go ahead, get a good look."

On Chet's insistence, Roman inched forward, finally getting a glimpse of the contents. *What?* He was looking at a golden lattice crust pie. What did a pie have to do with fertilizer price negotiations? Scratching his head, he was more confused than ever. He looked back at Chet, who nodded his head and wore a grin.

Lexi nodded at Mike. "Cherry-berry."

While Lexi sat down with Mike, Roman turned toward Chet. "*This* is how the fertilizer price is determined?" He heard the disbelief in his voice.

Chet chuckled. "I'm afraid so. It started…oh, maybe ten years ago by Lexi's grandfather. She often came along with him on these visits, but there was a time she presented him with a pie. After that, Dad said they'd have to find a reason for her to make him a pie at least once a year. For whatever reason, they agreed the fertilizer price was it."

Roman tilted his head back and chuckled. "That has to go down into the books. By the way, I noticed a sign for a B&B out front when we drove in."

Chet nodded. "My wife Andrea handles that now."

"Is that right?" Roman exhaled. So, Chet *is* married.

Chet nodded. "She loves it. Created a thorough marketing plan and now has it booked for most of the year. When we decided to expand our business by hosting weddings in the renovated pole barn, our business income boomed. It's a lucrative little side business for us. In fact, ours was the first wedding held in the new building."

"No kidding. I was just about to suggest hosting weddings to Lexi to help bring in additional revenue."

"We max out at five hundred guests," Chet said.

"Who would have thought so many couples would want to get married in Door County?"

"I know, right? We started referring out the smaller weddings. If you'd like, I can put Cherry Orchard on our referral list."

"I'll speak to Lexi about it right away, but I like the idea." This was the exact influx of revenue Cherry Orchard could use. Now, he'd have to convince Lexi, and he wasn't sure how that conversation would go. He knew by now she wasn't a fan of change.

"So, what do you think about using the pellets? Sound good?" Chet asked.

"I'm hoping it'll do what you say it will, but the course is in such a bad way. I'm a little concerned."

"It's not the product," Chet said.

"If it's not the fertilizer, then why is the course in such disrepair? There are actual bald spots in many of the open fairways. A good handful of greens suffered a complete wipeout, the fescue got blown away, and the fairways became thin. It must leave golfers questioning the state of the course."

"I can answer that," Lexi said, as she walked in their direction. "My grandfather made some cuts."

Chet nodded. "Your grandfather backed off on many things, even though I warned him that fertilizer shouldn't be one of them. He had his own mind. Bless his soul."

"Now it makes sense," Roman said, but a call over the walkie-talkie interrupted him before he could make his point.

Roman turned his back to the group and answered the distress call. "Eduardo, slow down and tell me what's going on. I can't understand you."

"We got a problem, Boss. The loader is sinking. You'd better come quick."

Roman completed the call and locked eyes with Lexi. "I'm sorry to interrupt Lexi, but we need to go right now."

Chapter 10

Roman and Lexi jumped back into the haul truck after making new arrangements for the fertilizer pickup. At the wheel, Roman tore out of Taylor Farms parking lot. He saw Chet's wave goodbye in the rearview mirror. Having heard part of the conversation, Chet told Roman to contact him right away if he needed his help. That didn't surprise Roman. Like all the other people Roman had met, Chet proved to be another stand-up guy.

Ten minutes later, they arrived on the scene. Having radioed Eduardo on the ride home, Roman knew exactly where to go…the retention pond near hole eight.

His stomach dropped when he spotted the backhoe in the water. With Eduardo behind the wheel, the engine growled. Water banged hard against the cab doors. They needed to be careful, or Eduardo might end up trapped inside like a bird in a cage. A cage that was sinking.

Lexi squeezed Roman's arm. "Oh, no. What's Eduardo doing?"

Roman pinched his lips between his teeth and then said, "He's trying to ground the machine so he can back it out. I've got to get in there."

"What? You? Shouldn't we call the fire department?"

"I can handle this," Roman said, not having the luxury of time to explain any further. He waded through the water toward the sinking machine. His steps slogged through the mud. His boots grew heavier with each step. He hoisted his body up onto the machine and opened the cab door.

Eduardo jerked his head toward Roman. Panic swam in the young employee's eyes. "I'm sorry, Boss, but when I saw the water leaking through…I…I just wanted to fix it quick."

Roman's heart softened. Along with ground maintenance, Eduardo had taken a special interest in the sand bunkers and fescue. It made sense that he'd include the retention pond in that group, but this situation was way out of his realm. "You did the right thing, but I've got it from here. Let me in there."

As they changed positions, Roman knew there was zero room for error. *No mistakes.* Beads of perspiration ran across Roman's forehead as he heard his father's voice whisper in his ear. *You'll never amount to anything. You're nothing but a screwup.* He stood frozen in time.

"Boss? Boss?" He heard Eduardo calling out to him, waiting for his instruction.

Roman cleared his head from the negative thoughts and slid behind the controls. The treated lumber they'd picked up the other day was still on the truck back at the shop. The extra weight could help pull this rig out of the jaws of the muck.

"Eduardo, go back to the shop and bring the truck

with the lumber on it. And bring a chain. I'll try to hold her steady until you get here."

Eduardo nodded and bolted for his vehicle while Roman steered his attention back to the problem at hand. He had a sinking heavy-duty piece of equipment on his hands that he was responsible for. He'd cut his teeth on a piece of equipment just like this one. The control deck had always felt like a second skin.

Roman wrapped powerful hands around the controls and dug the backhoe bucket as deep as he could into the mud. Then he dove the front-end loader into the sod to stabilize the machine and stop its descent. Betting against the odds, Roman hoped he could stop the sinking machine. But gravity won that bet, causing a slide even further into the muddy water.

Roman felt beads of perspiration run across his forehead. "Come on now, girl. Be good." He gritted the words between his teeth. Another descent and the ten-thousand-pound machine sank even further.

This wasn't working. Roman jerked his head and checked the back end. The wheels had completely submerged. Cursing under his breath, his experience warned him that any movement would make matters worse.

"Roman. Get out of there. Eduardo's on his way." Roman heard Lexi's plea, but he wouldn't stop trying, not yet. It wasn't who he was.

"Come on, Boss, it's sinking," came another request from the group, but Roman knew there had to be someone behind the wheel when Eduardo got back with the truck.

Water found its way into the cab. She was losing ground. When it tilted sideways, Roman's instincts knew it was too late. He surveyed the area for signs of Eduardo, but he was nowhere in sight.

The water level inside the cab began to rise. For a moment, Roman hesitated. He didn't want to have to do what he was about to do, but he'd run out of choices. His injured foot would be screamin' later, but having few options left him pinned in a corner. Now that Roman had made the decision, he leaned back, brought his knees to his chest, tightened his strong thighs and kicked the front windshield with his powerful legs.

Ping! The windshield flew out of its encasement in one piece, slid off the hood of the tractor, and into the water. Roman's biggest fear had all the makings of coming true. If the tractor slipped too far into the water and killed the engine…Roman grimaced, the rescue effort would be far more difficult.

Don't feed your fears, he reminded himself and lifted his body out of the cab. Shifting his weight to balance, Roman now stood on the roof of the engine, causing the machine to shift once again. He turned his attention to the road. *Where's Edwardo?*

A slip of the boot caused Roman to lose his balance. Backstepping to regain his foothold didn't help. He fell backward off the machine and into the mucky pool. Water as brown as his leather gloves hit his eyes and filled his mouth. The very water he'd been trying to avoid. When he popped up to the surface, he saw Eduardo tearing down the road. *Help me, Lord.* He had to get back up and onto that machine.

~

Lexi's heart hammered against her chest. She couldn't concentrate on the next step because she had no idea what that would be. She watched as Roman tried to wrangle the beast-like machine from sinking further into the water. Her grandfather had the retention pond built with a specific purpose in mind. A major component of the irrigation system, it would function as a collection pool. Over the last ten years, the tiered wall had begun to show signs of strain, growing weaker from rotted wood and decay, and Lexi suspected, placing the nearby holes at risk of flooding if it broke.

Lexi stared at the scene in front of her. The machine was fighting every attempt Roman made to dislodge it from the mud. Like a petulant child, it seemed to grind its hind tires deeper into the muck. Roman swiveled in the seat, moving his attention to the bucket.

Moments later, Lexi's heart sank when the front windshield broke free from the machine. It was over. Roman wasn't going to be able to free the loader on his own. Then, as if the situation couldn't get any worse, it just did when Roman slipped off the machine and into the water. Lexi bolted. If anything happened to him...

Mick wrapped a strong hand around her forearm. "Hey, wait a minute, Lexi, where are you going?"

Ignoring the warning in his voice, Lexi broke free and ran toward Roman with Mick on her heels. "What if he hit his head before he hit the water?" she hollered over the growl of the engine.

Roman surfaced. Water spewed from his mouth and nose. Once out of the pond, he stood to his full height, soaked and dirty, but still with that determined look of his on his face. That much hadn't changed.

"I'm okay." He waved his hand, then slicked his hair back.

Mick, now at Lexi's side, gave Roman's back a hard *thump.*

"Wow! Big guy," Roman teased, now bent over, his hands on his thighs.

At the sound of his voice, Lexi's entire body lost its edginess but it wasn't until he gave her a quick smile that her heart slowed back to normal.

Mick piped up with a suggestion. "We should probably take some pictures and contact the insurance company." He retrieved his smartphone from his pocket and started flipping through the apps.

Lexi's shoulders fell. "I suppose you're right." Even though the machine couldn't be saved, at least it was insured.

Roman raised a hand. "Wait a minute. "Let's see if we can't clean her up ourselves before filing a claim. Once you do that, the company will probably raise your premium. Eduardo, let's hook up the chain and get her out of this mud." Chain in hand, Roman started walking back to the water.

He never looked more in control of the situation, or more handsome. Lexi had finally found the answer to the question that haunted her.

He cared.

Chapter 11

With last week's crisis over, Roman awoke with a brand-new idea to put the golf course back at the forefront of the community's minds. For the last week, he'd split the crew into two camps. One was instructed to take apart the backhoe, clean the engine of mud and silt with power washers, and change all the fluids. The other he instructed to get started on the retaining wall rebuild.

With those tasks now completed, he walked into the clubhouse ready to lay out his big idea but was quickly deflated when Lexi turned to face him. By the look of her expression, something was wrong. He could feel it too.

"What is it?" He feared bad news about the loader and hoped one of the crew hadn't burdened her with some trivial problem. The last he'd determined was that no water had reached the engine, which meant they'd lucked out. A good hydraulic system flush and brand-new oil would do the trick.

He rested his arms on the bar and peered into her beautiful eyes that had captivated him for some time now. Inwardly he scowled, uncertain when that had happened. A new feeling overwhelmed him … a desire to fix whatever was wrong took precedence over everything else, even the list in his notepad paled.

Lexi sighed. "Uncle Bill stopped by last night."

Roman winced, glad it wasn't an issue with the backhoe but expecting bad news from the tone of Lexi's voice. "I noticed a car in the parking lot last night, but never gave it a second thought." By the look on Lexi's face, maybe he should have.

"I'm hoping he was just paying you a nice visit." So far, it didn't sound too serious to Roman.

The look in her eyes told him he was wrong with that assumption. "His realtor found them a condo in the Florida Keys."

Knowing Lexi's uncle was eager to sell his shares, this news added another layer of unwanted stress for her and her sisters. "I think I know what's coming next."

Lexi crossed her arms in front of her. "If you guessed they want to buy the condo, you're right."

Now what? Roman had to find a way to resolve this situation despite another hurdle that would have to be jumped. "And he needs his money sooner than expected?"

Lexi nodded. "He said by the middle of June would be," Lexi air quoted, 'ideal'.

"Hmm. I might have a solution. Chet told me all about the weddings they started hosting in their newly remodeled barn."

Lexi smiled, and the worry from a moment ago washed away from her face. "Did he tell you that their wedding was the first one held at the barn?"

Roman nodded. "He did."

"I was at their wedding. It was so lovely. A mix of straw bales and fine china, if you can imagine it."

Roman saw the open door to share his idea and decided to walk through it. "Chet suggested opening up the clubhouse here at Cherry Orchard and doing the same."

Lexi took a step back. "Us?"

Just as he expected, Roman spotted the resistance in Lexi's eyes but had grown used to her initial response to most new ideas. Her logical approach to most situations held a bit of caution with each change he'd suggested. He raised his hands to downplay the idea. "I think it's something we should consider as a supplemental income. Couples are now required to put down a substantial down payment to hold the date."

Lexi frowned, and Roman guessed she wasn't crazy about the idea.

"We don't know a thing about that industry. I'm not sure how much change we can handle all at once."

"You mean you're not sure how much *you* can handle?" Roman was pressing her, but she had to get used to the idea of leading the initiative for change. It'd be the only way Cherry Orchard would survive.

"We've changed so much already, and hosting weddings has nothing to do with golf."

Roman took a step back. "You're right. We'd be opening up the golf course to more of a venue, but I want you to focus on the extra income. The *immediate* extra income we'd see in the down payments."

"How would we even begin accommodating a wedding request?"

"By following Chet's lead. He offered to share their software and their vendor list so we could get started on the right foot. Apparently, Andrea has all the information stored on her hard drive."

"I admire your enthusiasm, Roman, but that's only part of the equation. We don't have a full kitchen. Most couples want to offer their guests a beautiful dinner. As you know by now, we don't have a full kitchen."

"Get this. Chet mentioned a new trend that more and more couples are opting for. Food trucks. Guests can order whatever they want and it's less expensive for the family."

Lexi's eyes widened in disbelief. "A food truck? Like the kind that sells cotton candy at the fair?"

Roman chuckled. "A lot nicer than that. But, I'm telling you, it's the latest and greatest in weddings. You'd be setting a brand-new trend in Door County. Some people may end up calling you a trendsetter."

Lexi gave Roman a playful shove. "You have an answer for everything."

"That's what you're paying me for."

"You're right, but you've far exceeded your wage. Are you still actively looking for a course you can pick up?"

Roman nodded. "I am and I'm not. Cherry Orchard takes priority. I've pushed everything else to the back."

"Hmm. I appreciate that as long as it doesn't stop you from your own dreams."

Roman shook his head. That's exactly what he'd done. Even though his realtor had been feeding him leads, it didn't feel right to take time away from Cherry Orchard. His dreams would have to wait. "Chet mentioned a destination wedding show coming up," he said, doing his best to change the subject. "Let's try to get in on that."

"Wait a minute. Are you saying you'd come with me?"

He gazed up at Lexi, reading the uncertainty in her eyes. How many times did he have to reassure her he'd be there for her? "Of course, I'll go. We're a team."

The relief he saw in her eyes touched him. She still needed him and honestly, that felt pretty good.

"Ellie's always up on the current events in the community. Let me reach out to her. I'm sure we're well past the deadline, but maybe she can pull some strings for us and get us in," Lexi said.

"Good thinking. Now that we've cleaned up the parking lot, we can take some nice photos of the clubhouse and the course and create a moving slide show. Couples will love to be able to see the grounds so they can visualize their wedding there."

Lexi nodded. "I'm excited."

"We need to continue brainstorming for extra revenue. This is a good example of doing just that," Roman said.

"This might shock you, but I had an idea that I wanted to run by you."

"I'm all ears. Let's hear it." This was exactly what Roman hoped would begin happening to Lexi—to act more like an owner.

"What if we took advantage of the holidays that fall during the season and offered a scramble or best ball event?"

Roman beamed. "Now you're thinking like a consultant. If I'm not careful, you could put me out of a job."

Lexi chuckled. "Hardly."

"I'm serious, Lex. That's an ideal way to kick off the summer starting with Memorial Day Weekend. Are there fireworks on the fourth of July?"

"We've had a traditional employee party on the fourth. At nine p.m. we shoot off fireworks. It's a big hit."

"How would they feel opening up the show to the public?"

"If it would benefit Cherry Orchard, I'm sure they'd be on board."

"We could take advantage of the opportunity and sell an all-day ticket. Do you have a grill?"

Lexi frowned. "A grill? There might be one in the back shed. Not sure if it works or not."

"I'll take a look at it."

Lexi shook her head.

"What?" Roman asked.

"All I'm going to say is that I shouldn't be surprised."

~

Later that evening, Lexi wondered if there was anything Roman couldn't do. From trying to save a heavy piece of equipment from total submersion to coming up with new revenue ideas for the course. His skill set was so varied and fine-tuned it was hard not to be impressed. And his soft side helped her rediscover humor in life again. Maybe Roman Hart dropped out of the sky, or was the knight in shining armor Ellie had suggested he was. Someone above was looking out for her when Roman walked into her life and she knew exactly who that was. *Thank You, Lord, for always looking out for me and for always being there.*

She smiled to herself as she completed her nightly walk around the golf course, tonight without Roman. Contentment filled her as she thought about all they'd accomplished since she'd hired him. They'd remodeled the golf course, repaired the parking lot, filled the woodpecker holes, repainted the clubhouse, and spread the chicken manure fertilizer. When she received the news that the loader would be back in action after a thorough cleaning, she knew she had received a blessing. Life was good at Cherry Orchard Golf Course. She hoped her grandfather was looking down and, more importantly, was pleased.

Her twilight walks had a way of soothing her soul from the day's work, and tonight was no exception. Usually Roman joined her, but tonight he told her he had to return a few calls and tend to some bookwork he could no longer ignore. She peered over at the guest cottage when she reached the last hole, wanting to knock on his door and ask him to sit for a while on the two adorable slingback chairs on the porch. He was so easygoing, making it impossible not to learn from him. But it had become more than that. Much more. She cared for Roman.

With the next kick of wind, an uncomfortable thought probed Lexi's pleasant thoughts. *He'll eventually leave.* Roman told her he'd been actively looking for a golf course, but it never worked out. Odd, Lexi thought. She would've thought at least one would have made the cut.

The first droplets of a rain shower fell. She hustled to her vehicle but gave the guest cottage one last look. Lights still flickered inside. Now that she knew him better, she pondered if he was his own worst enemy.

Punishing himself for blowing an athletic scholarship and messing up the future he was supposed to have. That would explain why he was still looking for a course. Was it possible there was a place down deep inside of him that believed he didn't deserve it? That would explain a lot.

Lexi's heart ached. If her suspicions proved true, the right course would never come.

Chapter 12

Roman stepped into the bowling alley, allowing his eyes to adjust to the dim lighting. He'd been looking forward to the annual bowling party Lexi had invited him to all week. It had been too long since he'd taken time off to have fun, and he couldn't remember the last time he'd bowled. Similar to Lexi, he'd devoted the last ten years to building his career. His goals were simple but clear and he was on track.

Taking in the dense, familiar scents of alley oil and an era of stale cigars, the place reminded him of his youth. Like his father, Roman had played in leagues, winning a tournament or two. The trophy that meant the most was one from the Father and Son Tournament shortly after he'd turned sixteen.

Roman arrived early, wanting to get a feel for the place. Sliding onto a stool, he ordered a drink and then positioned himself for a perfect view of the lanes. *Hmm, almost a full house.* He watched the bowlers release their balls and studied how they reacted as they rolled toward the pins. If the alleys were heavily oiled, a ball could spin out. If too dry, an extra punch was needed when it left the bowler's fingers. Roman smiled. Come to think of it, his right hook might come in handy, especially if he landed splits, hoping to pick up a spare. He rubbed his chin, happy to have remembered that hidden little gem.

As he sipped from his drink, his thoughts turned to Cherry Orchard. With most of the repairs winding down and new systems in place, his time at the golf course would soon come to an end. Typically, he'd be ready to wrap up the loose ends and start brainstorming for the next job, but something felt off. He wasn't in any particular hurry to leave.

This perplexed Roman. Was it possible he was tired of the nomadic lifestyle? Or, had he gone soft and allowed himself to get attached to the people here? Roman snickered thinking of Mick and his burly approach to every task and Eduardo and his team and how hard they were working toward maintaining the new directives. Then there was Lexi. Roman threw his head back as he downed the rest of his beverage, wishing he could just as easily wash down his feelings for her. He'd gone and made his life complicated.

He rose from the stool, hearing his name called out. "Roman, over here."

Searching the large area, he found Lexi waving him over to the other side of the room. He waved back, feeling on top of the world. Odd, he just saw her yesterday. Roman sluffed away the question in his head, paid the tab, and headed in her direction. When he reached her, he noticed the bowling shirt she wore had her name embroidered in the upper corner. *Adorable.*

He grinned, nodding to her shirt. "You a regular here?"

She shrugged. "I used to be. I see you found the place okay."

"Yup. I spotted it the first day I arrived. I was a league player as a kid. Now I like to throw a few balls to let loose and blow off some steam."

Lexi's mouth gaped. "Me too."

Roman widened his eyes. That was hard to believe. "Really?"

She waved off the misunderstanding. "No. I mean … not to blow off steam … but I used to bowl on a ladies' league Tuesday nights." She pointed to the logo stitched corner of her shirt. "When I started working a lot of overtime at the store, I had to quit."

"But you hung onto the shirt? Smart move. Odd coincidence, isn't it? We both bowled but decided to give it up because of our careers?"

She scrunched up her nose causing Roman's grin to widen. He loved it when she did that. "I guess it is." She scanned the room, probably searching for the others. "Did you have a chance to rent a pair of shoes yet?"

Roman shook his head. "I was too busy watching the lanes."

Lexi threw him a suspicious look. "Oh, I get it. You're already trying to get the upper edge, huh?"

He followed her to the shoe rental room. "I hope you don't have your hopes up to win today, do you?" He loved hearing her laugh as if she didn't have a care in the world. A bit of a dare usually got her going. "Because if you are, I think you're in for a bit of a surprise."

Lexi whirled around. Her eyes sparkled. "You're on!"

When more of the crew piled in, the group moved to the two reserved lanes and drew the three-person teams. It was decided that Roman would lead one team while Lexi the other. The aroma of pizza filled the air as a group of kids threw quarters into the air hockey game nearby. The sound of bowling balls hitting the lanes struck a familiar chord for Roman. Memories flooded back settling him into familiar territory and the new job details his uncle had sent him last night in an email was the furthest thing on Roman's mind.

He rubbed the palms of his hands together, generating warmth in his fingers for the first throw. He knew using a relaxed swing was key. He thoughtfully counted out his steps. Sliding forward on his left leg, he fully extended his right arm and focused on the third arrow on the right. It was a practiced, well-grooved-in set of movements that he was relying on for a strike from his league playing days.

As the games progressed, the flat screen above displayed the scores, keeping the teams informed of their standing with every ball thrown. The pressure was on. When the tenth frame came up in the third game, Roman zeroed in on his concentration.

"You're not going to win," Lexi teased from her lane.

"It'll be a challenge." Roman shot her a quick smile. He couldn't remember the last time he'd enjoyed himself as much as he had today. He'd have to thank her again for inviting him. His team was down, and Lexi was right, it wouldn't be easy to pull ahead unless he could nail this last ball.

He took his approach, counted out his steps, and let the ball go. Roman fought to remain calm despite his hammering heart as he watched his ball roll down the lane.

Ping, ping, ping, ping. The pins exploded picture perfect to the back of the pen. He threw his fist into the air but slowly let it drop to his side when two pins refused to fall. The four and the six. Now, he needed a spare.

"Better luck next time, big guy," Mick said, clearly the best player on Lexi's team.

Roman shot him a nod and retraced his steps to the ball return. He pasted on a false smile. "Don't count us out yet." He knew picking up a spare when you were looking at this type of splits was one of the hardest shots to pull off. He needed his hook now more than ever.

Shaking his hands to loosen his fingers, Roman held them over the fan and waited for his ball. "Finally," he muttered, for only his ears, when it popped up and rolled toward him. Perspiration dotted across his forehead as he picked up the ball, slid his fingers and thumb into the holes, and stared down the alley. *Patience.* When the conversations behind him about the tough shot he had begun to blur, he knew he'd slipped into the zone.

Roman steered his gaze to the right side of the six pin. If he could ride the right side of the lane, the ball would glaze the six pin, causing it to slide in the direction of the four pin, knocking it down. It had been a long time since he'd pulled off a throw like this, but it was in him. All he had to do was believe in himself.

Four steps later, he slid into position, extended his strong arm, and gave the ball an extra quarter turn to engage the hook and threw it down the lane.

The laughter started first deep in his belly. By some miracle, he'd made the shot! He heard Lexi's whoop behind him. When he turned around, he found both teams, mouths aghast, looking at him like he was a bowling guru.

"I don't know where that came from." Roman tried his best to defend himself against the groans from Lexi and her teammates. He leisurely walked back to his side of the alley toward his teammates who welcomed him with hefty thumps on the back. The event couldn't have ended any better.

After the shoes were returned and the balls were placed back on the racks, Roman walked toward the exit with the others. He felt a fist pump on his shoulder, turned toward the culprit, and found a grinning Mick.

"Glad to have you on board, buddy. You really evened us out, until we realized you were a ringer!" Mick chuckled.

"I had a ball," Roman said, causing more groans than laughter at the pun he thought of using at the last minute.

"Thanks for buying the pizza in the fifth frame," Eduardo added before darting out the door.

As Roman waited for Lexi to settle the bill, he thought about how well the afternoon had gone. Not for the winning throw he'd managed to pull off but for the privilege of meeting such a fine group of people. *Do they realize how lucky they are?* Roman's introspection turned humble. He stared at the shoes on his feet. A new truth took hold somewhere deep in his gut. He wanted the permanence of friends and family back in his life.

When Lexi turned and made her way to the exit, the look on her face told Roman she was pleasantly surprised to find him waiting for her.

"May I walk you to your car?" he asked.

Lexi smiled. "I'd like that."

Roman held her coat, and she slid her arms into the sleeves and buttoned it up. "This was fun tonight. Thanks for including me. There never seems to be enough time to relax and enjoy. My life has become a giant rat race, running from job to job."

Lexi stepped out into the twilight-lit sky and Roman followed. "That's part of my life I decided to change when we inherited Cherry Orchard but for the same reason. I was on the road to burnout."

"Regrets?"

Lexi shook her head. "Not a one. The long hours I put in have readied me for Cherry Orchard, along with your mentorship, of course."

"You sound as if we've crossed the finish line. We're not done yet." Roman teased.

Lexi chuckled. "Good. I'm ready for whatever comes next. I'm not afraid of change anymore after being thrust into decision-making by force."

Roman grinned, enjoying their banter as always. "The only way you're going to learn how to swim is to get into the water."

Their laughter mingled as they turned the corner and in doing so, faced the wind coming off the Bay. Roman felt the bite in the air on his cheeks first. He slid the scarf from his neck and turned to Lexi, causing her steps to slow. Wrapping it around her neck, he tugged her toward him and gave her a sheepish smile. It was impossible not to capture her gaze. A desire to take care of her hit him hard. He hadn't expected this reaction from his playful gesture. His thoughts swam between the life he'd made for himself and the one he now wanted.

Roman swallowed down his tug-of-war thoughts. Lexi was still looking at him, still smiling. Finally, he said, "It's … uh…a little chilly out here. Thought you may like this."

She tucked the scarf securely around her neck. Her smile widened, drawing him closer.

He inched toward her. Their coats rubbed against each other. Her breath mingled with his. *One kiss? Would that hurt?*

"Thank you, Roman ... the scarf ... that's very thoughtful," she murmured.

Roman faltered. Her words reeled him backward in time. He pulled away from the rare moment as fast as he'd given in to his feelings. He tried to ignore the trigger that always re-opened the back door to the truth ... to the man he *really* was ... the screwup.

"Thoughtful? Me?" If he had thought of his *father's* feelings the night of the accident, he wouldn't have ended up hurting all the people he loved the most. A familiar, unwanted guest, regret, roared in and found its place snugly between them.

Lexi slowed her steps.

Had she noticed his sudden spell of sullenness? He could feel her watching him.

He felt the light touch of her hand on his shoulder. "Roman? Are you okay?"

Roman pushed the negative funk aside. He was spending time with Lexi and that time was dwindling. It wouldn't be long and he'd be on the road again to the next job. That's where men like him belonged ... on the move. Not in little villages like Sister Bay where friends could rely on him and a wife to welcome him home.

Give me the strength, Lord. He plastered a smile on his face that didn't match his feelings. "I'm okay," he lied. "I was just thinking about how wonderful you are with your employees. I've worked in a lot of different places around the Midwest, and I can tell you that what you've created here is rare. You interact with them more like a family than a boss."

As insightful as she was, Lexi let the uncomfortable moment slide, even though she must've been questioning what had happened a moment ago.

"I must've learned by osmosis how to treat the employees by watching my grandfather. That was his rapport with his staff, but when he had to be stern, he was. I'm not looking forward to that role."

"Makes sense that you'd follow in his footsteps."

"If he were here with us right now, he'd ask you a question."

Roman raised his eyebrows, feeling a bit off-put by her suggestion. "Oh? And that would be?"

"Are you ever planning to settle down in one place and find that golf course you need?"

Roman pressed his lips together in a hard line. It had been a long time since he'd opened up to anyone on this topic, but tonight felt different. He could trust Lexi. If she had questions about him, he wanted to answer them.

"After I lost the scholarship, it was easier to stay away. I couldn't bear to see the disappointment in my father's eyes. The hardest decision I made was to keep a distance between us, to walk away for a while. Teaming up with my uncle was one of the best decisions I made after the accident. I'm always on the go, never in one place for very long."

When he turned to her, he saw the sadness in her turned-down eyes.

His heart pulled. "I'm sorry. I should keep that stuff to myself."

Her hand touched his shoulder. "That breaks my heart, but I'm glad you told me. It answers some questions I had about you."

Roman found it intriguing that she had been thinking about him long enough to stir her curiosity. "You had questions about me? Like what?"

"How you avoid social gatherings. Remember your initial resistance to this bowling party invite? You've grown used to being alone, haven't you?"

Roman shrugged a shoulder. "I suppose I have." He narrowed his eyes, sharpening his focus on the past. She was right. He'd become accustomed to a single life, even though he'd always dreamed of settling down one day and having a family. Like any regular guy would.

"Is forgiveness part of this equation?"

Roman didn't hesitate. He knew the answer to that question. "I don't think my dad's interested. Maybe after he sees what I've done with my life. What I've accomplished. That's why I…"

Lexi interrupted. "I didn't mean from your father. I meant for yourself. Maybe that's why you're just working a job instead of what God intended you to do with the gifts He gave you."

~

Like the predictability of a pendulum's movement, Lexi waited patiently, not wanting to interrupt Roman's thoughts. If she were right, he had a misconception about himself, a big one. One mistake doesn't define a man's life but teaches the greatest life lesson. For reasons she didn't understand and would not question, Lexi believed God was using her to step into the muddied waters of Roman's life. But she had to move cautiously.

"Are you suggesting I'm holding myself back?"

She gave him a leveled gaze, picking up on a slight tone of irritation in his voice. She knew she'd landed on a piece of the truth.

Roman gave her a sideways glance. "I've been working on my program for years, waiting for the right course to present itself. Waiting on God's timing."

Roman's defense was solid. It was also well rehearsed and grooved into a smooth shine to keep him right where he was. "Maybe He's given you the tools to put the program together but expects *you* to step into the future with it."

She heard the frustrated breath leave his lips. "And that's what I'm doing. Keeping an eye out for the right golf course. A course I can afford."

Lexi knew her next question would press Roman. "Are you?"

"I'm not following." His curt tone rubbed the edge of Lexi's point. He would whittle it down if she gave him half the chance. That's the mechanism he'd been using all these years. The one that told him he didn't deserve a thing, and he'd better be careful not to mess things up again. It kept him refining the program and looking for that elusive golf course. Most of all, it silenced him to be satisfied.

"I see your lights burning into the night, and I know you're working on the program. I'm sure you have the three-ring binders to prove it." Lexi heard his light chuckle, giving her the courage to keep going. "Coming up with new ideas to replace your already good ideas isn't difficult for a man who's stuck."

Roman lifted his head to the star-studded sky. After a moment he said, "I'm *not* stuck."

"You haven't taken the next step by presenting the program to people who could help spread the word or even garner sponsors who might be interested in investing. You're swimming in circles around an idea. Maybe it's time to bring it out of the shadows and trust in what you've created."

Lexi pulled her key fob from her coat pocket and signaled the unlock. Roman stepped forward and opened the door for her. "You really believe this?"

She peered into the eyes of this hardworking, tortured man. How could she fill him with the strength he needed to step forward in life even though it might take him out of hers?

She raised a hand and brushed his face with a light touch, wanting to bring him into her arms and fill him with the confidence he so desperately needed.

"Yes, Roman, I do."

Chapter 13

Lexi surveyed the expansive hall hosting the Door County Destination Wedding Show and questioned if she and Roman had made the right decision to attend. Surrounded by some of the largest wedding venues in the county, her little golf course on the Bay seemed like a minnow in big fish waters.

She was thankful for Ellie pulling strings to get them added as a vendor … but *squeezed in* were the appropriate words. With their table side-angled into a corner, it looked every bit the last-minute addition.

Lexi put a stop to her negative thinking. Even one booking would be a positive outcome and worth their while. She unfolded a cherry red tablecloth, spreading it across the six-foot folding table that was provided with the one-hundred-dollar registration fee. The organizers suggested offering a presentation and not to forget a wrapped sweet to draw the attendees to their table. Lexi had packed both.

When everything was complete, Lexi glanced at her

watch. Her heart pitter-pattered against her chest. There was still plenty of time to set up, but where on earth was Roman? She noticed the long line of couples waiting for the doors to open. Without warning, her stomach tightened. Was it the third cup of coffee she'd had in place of breakfast? No, she knew what it was.

He's not going to show.

The threatening thought swirled in her head like a waterspout on the Bay. A familiar sense of dread slithered in, clamping its hold on her. She found one of the chairs through blurred vision, grabbed the arm, and fell into the chair.

No. No. No. Not now. Not here. Lexi closed her eyes and concentrated on her breathing, a meditation technique that sometimes worked to ward off the wretched memory. *Breathe in, breathe out.*

It had been so long since the harsh disappointment had tormented her. She was foolish enough to assume it was gone for good.

But there she was. A middle schooler again. Dressed in a brand-new pink and white ruffled dress and her first pair of shiny, black strappy shoes.

Waiting.

He wouldn't forget. Not tonight. Her father had promised he'd take her to the father-daughter dance. Lexi was so excited to show her handsome dad off to all her girlfriends. He'd always looked so dashing dressed in his suit when he left for the office. The fathers would shake hands and the girls would smile.

When the gong of the grandfather clock signaled fifteen minutes past the hour, Lexi quickly filled in an excuse. He must've run into traffic. Her mother told her a few minutes late wouldn't be the end of the world.

They'd miss the principal's speech, welcoming all of them to the special evening. They could still make it to the grand march when all the young ladies would be announced with their fathers, but he had to walk through that door.

Thirty minutes. Sixty. Ninety.

No daddy.

Lexi felt warm tears tumble down her face.

Was she crying? When she opened her eyes, she saw Roman come into view. Bent on one knee, he was pressed up close, right next to her.

How embarrassing.

He laid his hands on her arms. The warmth was as comforting as that from a toasty fire on a cold day. It spread throughout Lexi's body. She couldn't help but lean into his strength, his touch.

"Lexi, are you all right?" Roman's face was so close to hers, shielding her from onlookers' gazes.

Wiping her cheeks dry with her hands, she gave him a half-smile. "Yes, of course. Just a silly memory. I'm glad you made it."

His eyes softened. "I said I'd be here. There was an accident on the highway. I had to take a detour. I'm sorry, Lex. You sure you're, okay?"

Lexi nodded, wishing she could place an ice pack on her flushed cheeks, hot with embarrassment. How she wished these episodes would slide off into the Bay. "We can talk about it later, but for right now, I'm fine, and I think we'd better get set up before we run out of time." She got to her feet and walked over to the pull cart Roman had brought with him.

"Okay. Let's do this," Roman said and started unbundling the boxes.

Lexi appreciated Roman's optimism that steered them through the awkward moment. He began removing the bungee cord around the boxes on the pull cart, but when the first warning bell rang thirty minutes later, Lexi panicked. "We're not ready."

Roman placed another wrapped gift box on top of the other, creating a pyramid of wedding presents to draw attention, and then climbed down from the small ladder. "No, we're not, but remember our motto, one step at a time. Did you remember the extension cord so we can get the PowerPoint presentation going?"

Lexi spun around and reached for the toolbox she'd packed up the night before. Pushing past the electrical tape, a small jar of screws, and a hammer, she pulled out a thick orange cord and handed it over to Roman.

Roman made quick work of plugging in the cord to the power source and the computer. "Okay, let's give this a go." He opened his laptop and ran his fingers across the keyboard. Nothing. He checked both connections and pressed the power button again.

Again, nothing happened.

From Lexi's viewpoint, it all looked to be in good condition. "Oh, no," she breathed.

"Now just hold on. Let's check the outlet and make sure we've got power. If we do, it's probably the cord."

"There's no spare," she whispered as if a panel of judges were lurking behind a curtain and would kick them out of the show for faulty equipment.

Sappy love songs piped in over the sound system. "Good morning, ladies and gentlemen, and welcome to the Door County Destination Wedding Show." A strong baritone voice boomed over the loudspeakers as the doors opened and the attendees poured into the building.

"What do we do now?" Lexi asked. "Should I run to the hardware store?"

"Looks like you folks could use some help." A middle-aged man with kind eyes and a Santa Claus white beard walked toward them, an extension cord in hand. Lexi read his name tag: *Dave, Murphy, Wedding Destinations.*

"Oh my gosh, yes, we could. Thank you," Lexi said. After seeing Dave's nametag, she reached for the magic marker and blank tags she was given when she arrived, and filled in their names. Releasing the adhesive back, she pressed hers onto the left corner of her sweater and handed one to Roman.

"Did anyone ever tell you that you have perfect timing?" Roman asked. He offered his hand and the two men shook.

"There was a first time for all of us. You're new to the group, aren't you?"

Lexi nodded. "We're a small, private golf course in Sister Bay. I'm Lexi and this is Roman. We decided to offer our venue for intimate weddings."

Santa pointed to his nametag. "I'm Dave," he said with a smile that would be fitting for any holiday. "You've come to the right place. I've been attending this event for the last ten years and have always done well with bookings for the entire year. Are you open to some advice?"

Roman accepted the cord from him. "You bet. It was my idea to try this, and I don't want Lexi to be disappointed," Roman said.

Lexi knew Roman had long ago learned the value of sound advice from those in the business. Over the years, he'd told her he'd picked up some valuable hints that he still used to this day.

Dave stepped closer. "Don't have the mindset of selling," He waited as if delivering the punchline to a great joke. Lexi didn't follow the stranger's thinking. They were all here to sell their venues so his advice didn't make sense.

Roman tilted his head. "Isn't that why we're here?"

Lexi looked at Roman and nodded. She wasn't the only one who wasn't following.

Dave grinned. "Get to know the people who approach your booth and you'll do a lot better. Act as if selling your venue to them for their wedding is merely a coincidence."

"You're taking the pressure off," Lexi said, appreciating the light bulb moment.

"Now you're getting it. Instead of pushing your venue, ask them how they got engaged or what they love the most about each other."

"I think I get it. Let them do the asking about what we offer, right?" Lexi asked.

Dave gave them a thumbs-up. "You do that and you'll be successful wherever you go."

By early afternoon, Lexi glared at their table from across the expansive room. *What's wrong?* They had so few attendees stop by their booth. The table decked out with a red tablecloth and white skirting made an attractive stop. They'd stacked heart-wrapped boxes on top of one another and placed a large cardboard cutout of Cupid and his arrow on top. Their chocolate fountain was pooling beautifully and the slide show was running continuously on the back wall. Lexi brought one of her prized possessions that her mother had given her, a crystal vase filled with pink and red foiled chocolates.

The only thing missing was some kind of lighting, but that couldn't be the problem.

Even though they applied Dave's advice, they hadn't made one solid transaction. Several couples approached their table, all preferring the smaller venue, but with no commitments. No down payments. Lexi didn't have time to produce a brochure, so she used her business card, front and back, to fill in the details. Was that the mistake? She was so out of her league here. All three couples smiled and told them they'd get back to them after the show. *Are they simply being polite?*

She smiled at Roman who decided to join her. "I know what that pretty little head of yours is thinking. It's not over until it is." He gave her an arm a light squeeze, pulling her out of the dumps.

Lexi sighed. "You're right but I hate this desperate feeling inside of me."

Roman lifted her chin so their eyes met. "What is it that's troubling you, Lex?" A desire to help her filled Roman so full it almost hurt.

Lexi fought a mountain of fear that surged inside of her. Everything was on the line—her future, Cherry Orchard's legacy, the employees. "That if this doesn't work, I'll fail and lose it all."

"You've stepped up, and that takes an incredible amount of strength. Embracing the future isn't easy for anyone. Give yourself a chance and give it some time."

Lexi smiled but always had trouble accepting compliments. This was no exception. Lights flickered overhead, signaling the attendees that the event was drawing to a close. "Are you still impressed even though we didn't book one wedding today?" she asked.

"You bet I am. We've got some strong nibbles.

That's good work for our first time trying the event," Roman said as he wound up Dave's extension cord.

Lexi gathered up the tablecloth and folded it into a neat square. "Have you always looked at things with such a positive spin?"

"Never hurts to carry one around. Maybe give it a try sometime." Roman chuckled, enjoying his sense of humor.

Lexi swung around. "Hey! Wait just a minute. Are you saying…"

"Is it too late to sign up?"

Lexi stopped her packing and spun around. A couple was heading over to their table.

Chapter 14

Roman recognized the look of surprise on Lexi's face when the couple walked toward their table. He probably wore a similar expression. Maybe their luck hadn't run out.

Lexi placed the tablecloth in a bin and stepped forward. "Not at all. How can we help?" she gushed.

Roman grinned at the excitement in Lexi's voice that bubbled over in enthusiasm. If only he could capture this moment and store it on a shelf for her.

The young man shifted his gaze in Roman's direction. That's when Roman spotted it. The intention in that young man's eyes … to make this work out for his bride-to-be. "We need a small venue for our wedding this July. I'm Luke Hunter and this is my fiancée, Cassie Hamilton."

Lexi stepped closer to the table. "The same Cassie Hamilton who owns The Perfect Cup Café?"

Cassie's smile widened. "That's right. Do we know each other?"

Lexi shook her head. "No, but I went to school with your high school quarterback brother, Conrad."

"And I've been enjoying coffee and croissants just about every morning," Roman added, patting his stomach.

Cassie chuckled. "What a small world. I'm glad to hear that you've been in the café."

"And you must be the new vet at Happy Paws?" Lexi asked, shifting the conversation to Luke.

"That's right," Luke said. "I took over the practice after my uncle retired and moved to Florida."

Cassie placed her hand on her chest. A pretty diamond ring sparkled under the fluorescent lighting. "We both have enjoyed playing golf at Cherry Orchard and fell in love with it. It's a stunning location. We didn't realize you were hosting weddings now."

"It's a brand-new venture for us and only for small, intimate weddings," Lexi said.

"That would be perfect and exactly what we want. When we heard you had a table here at the Show, we immediately set out to find you," Cassie said.

"But we got a little lost in this building," Luke added.

Cassie raised the laminated pamphlet that the attendees received when they arrived. "You're not listed in the brochure."

Roman nodded. "Sorry about that. We were late to register and didn't make the cut."

"Thank you for not giving up. We'd love to talk about hosting your wedding," Lexi said.

An announcement came over the speakers, drawing Roman's attention. "Vendors, we ask that you finish up if you are in the process of a booking. Attendees, we thank you for coming. Be sure you have all your belongings and promotional material you received today, and once again, congratulations on your engagements."

Roman wanted to curse. The announcement couldn't have been more ill-timed. He would've gladly paid another hundred-dollar entry fee to have thirty more minutes.

The soft ballads that had been playing in the background for the day went dead silent as the house lights switched over to a stark, high-beam setting. Roman didn't have a lot of sales experience, but he knew it was now or never to land this booking. He'd turned the job at Cherry Orchard over to God a long time ago, but the weaker side of him knew they needed a break. The renovations, the added pressure of buying her uncle's shares, and the loader repair expense all created a perfect financial storm for Lexi and her sisters. Maybe this was God's way of helping out.

He cleared his throat, drawing the attention of all three individuals. "I'd suggest starting with a set reservation, especially if you have a date your hearts are set on."

After turning to each other, Cassie and Luke smiled and remarked, "The third Friday in July."

Roman stepped over to the table and picked up the planner. The last Friday of July had a tentative hold from one of the other couples, but the twentieth was still open. The day they wanted. *Whew.* He liked this couple and wanted to accommodate their request. "It's still available if you want it."

Luke nodded. "Put us down. When can we come out and tour the grounds? We'd like to get the ball rolling and pay the down payment."

"How does Saturday sound?" Roman asked as he wrote their names in the planner, securing the date.

Lexi turned to Roman. "That's opening day."

Roman heard the concern in Lexi's voice. "Yes, the country club will be buzzing with activity. It'll be perfect and give Luke and Cassie a good feel of how it'll look and feel on their wedding day."

Lexi smiled. "Good thinking."

"Sounds good to us, right Cass?"

Cassie smiled. "Can't wait. Thank you both. We'll see you Saturday."

Once Cassie and Luke were out of earshot, Lexi twirled to face Roman. "We did it," she said. And it was then Roman saw in her eyes something he'd never seen before...trust. Finally, she trusted him. Roman clapped his hands together and then opened his arms.

Lexi easily breezed right into them.

He squeezed her tight, breathing in the faint scent of cherry blossoms in her hair. She felt wonderful in his arms like she belonged there.

"What a great way to end the day," he said.

She pulled away and smoothed her hair, even though there wasn't a strand out of place. "Yes, the absolute best."

Roman didn't want the day to end. He always believed in celebrating the little things in life. Why not now? "Let's finish packing up our gear and head out of here. Do you feel like grabbing a pizza?"

Lexi beamed. "I'd love that."

Thirty minutes later, after they placed an order at Kippy's Pizzeria and Wings, Roman's thoughts went back to how upset Lexi had been when he'd been late. "Care to talk about what happened earlier?" He wanted to understand what had upset her to the point of tears.

The relaxed gaze Lexi had a moment ago left her face. Roman instantly regretted his question.

Lexi turned away for a moment before her gaze settled back on Roman. "I tend to assume the worst-case scenario when I get in certain situations."

Roman nodded. "I've picked up on that much, but what I was looking at was a lot more serious. You were crying, Lex."

Lexi nodded. "That can happen in my weaker moments."

Roman forced his jaw closed. "This has happened before? Why?"

"Someone very dear to me made a habit of not showing up in my life."

"I take it this person was someone important?"

Lexi nodded. "My whole world." She gazed off into the room as if peering into the pool of the past. "As if I didn't matter at all. When you were late today…"

Roman's stomach dropped. "My being late must've stirred all that hurt up again." If only he had known. Now everything was beginning to make sense. Her reluctance to change, the hesitation to take the reins of the golf course, to the experience that happened to her today. It all linked back to this moment when she stopped believing in herself.

Lexi nodded, and Roman spotted a tinge of apple red on her cheeks. Now he'd embarrassed her. How could he help mend that broken part of her? He reached for her hand. "Life has a way of knocking us down, but it's how we learn from those times that helps us heal."

"You sound like a man who has had experience with that."

Roman nodded. A feeling so strong to fix what had broken inside of her moved him beyond his agenda for life. He knew he'd be gone soon, but felt compelled to help her. "I've made my share of mistakes in the past, but I deserved every consequence. It sounds like someone very important hurt you. I hope I can help close up that wound forever."

She gave her head a slight tilt and looked up at him with uncertainty in her eyes. If she had been just a little closer, he would have slipped his hand behind her head and put his lips on hers for the very first time. *What is happening here?*

"You?" she asked, pulling Roman out of their first almost imaginary kiss. The look of uncertainty only moments ago was replaced with a slight smile.

Roman threw her a relaxed smile, wondering if she'd read his thoughts. A feeling of being centered and whole and just plain good filled him, snuffing out all the old tapes that ran overtime in his head. "Yup. Me."

Chapter 15

At five a.m., Roman splashed tepid water on his face and prepared to shave. He had a hard time believing that the season opener had arrived. He smiled at the white polo shirt embroidered with *Cherry Orchard Golf Course* in the corner. Although he wasn't a permanent employee, Lexi insisted he was part of the Cherry Orchard family when she handed him the shirt. After all the contributions and hard work, she'd told him he'd earned it. He liked how that sounded…being part of a family again.

As Roman ran a comb through his unruly hair, he reviewed some of the major enhancements they had implemented on the course and clubhouse. The course was ready to show off its new turf, fertilized grasses, blooming fescue, and super-sized flower baskets.

It was Lexi's idea to add new signage to each tee box. Using a set of stencils, he helped her scroll out golf words of wisdom on each plaque. His favorite was on the fifth hole, a quote from Ben Hogan, "The most important shot in golf is the next one." Loving the game, Roman agreed with the master on that one.

All items on Roman's to-do list had been completed. The retention pond was now sound with new reinforced lumber and drainage tile. The loader was painstakingly cleaned and stored back in the shop. Broken sprinkler heads were replaced and now the grasses and fescue had perked up. Everything was primed and ready to go. So, the smile he wore on his face as he made his way over to the big event was fitting.

Walking through the clubhouse, feeling on top of the world, he popped a handful of chocolate candies into his mouth and then spotted Eduardo. He was outside on the patio, setting up the grill. Roman spotted a couple of coolers stacked high, a counter-height bench holding grilling utensils, and a roaster filled with sauerkraut for the bratwurst caught his eye. Next to a bowl of sweet onions and peppers, someone neatly lined up the condiments. Another table offered plates, napkins, utensils, and buns. *What a spread!*

Roman opened the door and peeked his head around the doorframe. "All set for today?"

"I'm in heaven. I don't think I've seen so many hot dogs and brats in my life." Eduardo chuckled and slipped a chef's apron over his head, tying the strings into a secure knot at his waist.

Roman gave him a thumbs up. "Don't forget the hat."

"You got it, Boss," Eduardo said and slipped the tall white chef's hat onto his head. Now he looked more the part.

Moving through the dining area, Roman found the wait staff busy placing decorated mason jars on the tables. When he spotted Lexi, his feet slowed. She was beaming as she welcomed the first set of golfers for the day. He'd never met the man, but he wished her grandfather could see her now. She was every bit in charge and his job at Cherry Orchard was finished. Roman's heart pinged. He knew this day was coming, bittersweet as it was.

Roman shook his head fighting a good dose of disbelief. With her hair tucked behind her head in a soft bun, it was hard to believe she could look any prettier than she always had, but she'd managed it. Loose tendrils brushed against her face, creating a wispy look to her. Roman leaned against the support beam in the room, kicked one boot over the other, and watched her delegate instructions for the day.

Lord, she doesn't need me anymore. A swift, melancholy breeze rushed through him when he realized he didn't want to go. The thought of never seeing Lexi again caused an ache deep inside his bones. He'd never know what could have been between them.

When Lexi turned to face him, she strode toward him. "Good morning."

Roman met her halfway. "Morning, Lex." He walked by her side as they strolled through the main dining area.

"We have Cassie and Luke arriving any minute to go over the details of their wedding."

"Here's the preliminary workout you and I put together." He handed Lexi a binder. "Are you planning to give them a tour of the grounds today?"

Lexi nodded, setting free a golden strand of hair from the bun. "Yes. Which reminds me. I spoke to Conrad. He's stopping over next week to take the measurements for the gazebo. There's a payment plan we can take advantage of...if we need it. But I think I should check with our bank. To compare rates." Then, as an afterthought, she said, "Right?"

Roman shook his head, impressed with his protégé. *She's already in charge.* "Good job getting Conrad on board right away." Anticipating his departure, Roman grimaced, fully aware that he would be gone by the time the gazebo went up. He'd never see its completion or anything else they'd planned for the season.

Lexi flipped through the wedding binder for Luke and Cassie. A subtle fragrance of her cherry blossom perfume wafted through the air. "Do you remember the two other couples we spoke with at the destination wedding show?"

Roman grinned. "Are you referring to the couples you said would probably never call?"

Lexi chuckled. "Well, I was wrong. They both called and booked their dates. We now have weddings in June, July, and August."

The lift in her voice set the sails of his melancholy mood out to sea, allowing him the luxury of basking in the good news. He was so proud of her. After a moment, Roman said, "You fit well in his shoes."

Lexi crinkled up her nose. "What ...whose shoes? As far as I can see, I'm wearing my own."

"Your grandfather's."

Lexi's eyes widened. "I...uh... hadn't thought of that. Thank you, Roman."

Roman shrugged. "If the shoe fits..."

Lexi giggled and gave Roman a playful shove.

Roman gave the room a quick scan, expecting she'd follow his gaze. "The place sure grows on you, doesn't it? I'll miss it."

"Why does this sound like a goodbye? Didn't anyone tell you that you can never leave us?"

Roman grinned but knew she understood by the look in her eyes. "When I arrived last month, you didn't know what to do first. Now look at you. You couldn't be more in charge."

Lexi chuckled, suggesting to Roman she was trying to lighten the moment.

"Oh, I'm not so sure about that. I'm pretty good at façade," she said.

Roman gave her a skeptical look. "No, you're not. You're beautifully transparent." His gaze spotted Cassie and Luke outside on the patio, talking easily with Eduardo. The trio was laughing, lightening Roman's heart. As if by premonition, he envisioned the future. Fireworks exploded in the sky, a bride and groom in an embrace, another wedding, another couple, a group of ladies finishing up league play and heading into the dining room for the lunch special. The images rolled through his head like a movie. That's when he knew for certain that Lexi was going to be okay. She was going to make it. But nowhere in this movie did he see himself.

"Why don't you go out and start the meeting without me? I want to make sure the brochures for my pilot program are strategically placed. We have some pretty important players showing up today."

Lexi shook her head and Roman knew she'd put up a fight on this. "But I'm sure they'll expect both of us at the meeting." Her tone wasn't argumentative, but firm. It also heard a subtle hint of the old insecurity he'd hoped was gone.

Roman needed to get this right. He wanted her to

remember, long after he was gone, that she was more than competent to do this job. "You can do this. It's your time."

A part of him wished she weren't ready. That she still needed him. The smile she gave him told him his intuition was right.

With a tilt of her head, she said, "Okay. But join us when you can."

"I need to get my brochures into the hands of the right people. Maybe I'll get lucky."

"I like this new initiative of yours but you don't need luck. That's what you told me. Your program is a winner. All you need is the right person. Maybe this is *your* time, too. One step at a time, remember?"

He pressed a smile on his lips and watched her walk away from him. He knew she wore a welcoming smile reflected on the faces of Cassie and Luke. When all three of them gazed in his direction, he assumed they asked about him. Certain Lexi used a smooth, diplomatic response, he was certain she probably explained that he was no longer needed, and she'd be in charge moving forward. *As it should be.* Roman's heart sank.

So why didn't he want to go?

Chapter 16

Lexi didn't understand Roman's reluctance to join her in the meeting. As she walked across the expansive room, her eyes caught the pretty design on the window treatments, thanks to Ellie's handiwork. She couldn't believe all the changes Cherry Orchard had undergone in such a short amount of time. Eduardo's crew now had a brand-new approach to maintaining the fairways, rough, and greens. The retaining wall and the irrigation had been repaired and Chet's fertilizer came through as promised, producing an emerald-green sheen across the entire property. Even the fescue grasses had flourished.

It was obvious that Mick was in heaven with the official starter booth that offered scoring cards, pencils, ball markers and tees. Two beverage cart servers joined the staff to ensure players would stay hydrated and to keep an eye on play—another excellent addition suggested by Roman.

The clubhouse also revealed many positive changes

that enhanced the club. A coat of fresh paint paired with Ellie's decorating additions added a splash of needed color and pizzazz. Even the new engineered wood flooring, a change Lexi fought long and hard against, had won her approval. Roman Hart had been the blessing Lexi never saw coming, or the knight in shining armor Ellie claimed him to be.

Lexi stepped out onto the deck and gave Luke and Cassie an energetic smile. Roman's encouraging words echoed in her head, casting away the doubts about herself. "Welcome, you two." She shook each of their hands in a warm greeting.

"Will Roman be joining us?" the bride-to-be asked. Her eyes searched for him through the brand-new windows Roman had installed.

Lexi's stomach pitched. She anticipated this question when Roman told her he wouldn't join them, yet he assured her that this was *her time*. Inhaling a steady breath, she led the way to her shared office with the storage pantry. "No, I'll be handling the wedding details from here. Let's sit in my office where it's more private."

For the next couple of hours, Lexi, Cassie, and Luke discussed the wedding ceremony, the food trucks, and a small two-piece band they wanted to add if they could swing it. Lexi suggested a conference call with Cassie's brother to ensure the gazebo would be ready, the site for exchanging their vows. When Lexi assured Cassie she could dance with her new husband under the stars, Lexi knew the meeting had gone well. Roman was right. Everything ran smoothly for her without a hitch. But where was Roman? He was supposed to join them after checking on the brochures.

After saying goodbye to the couple, Lexi went to the dining room when she heard Eduardo trailing her steps. "Miss Lexi, we have a problem."

Lexi turned to face a panic-stricken chef. She gave him a reassuring smile. "Yes, Eduardo."

"We ran out of hot dogs. What do you want me to do? Should I run to the grocery store?"

This was one of those minor problems her grandfather had solved on the spot. He had a roll-off-the-shoulders attitude, applying simple logic to solve most issues. She'd have to learn to do the same. Roman would tell her that her time to take the reins was right now.

Lexi glanced at her watch. It was nearing mid-afternoon, still plenty of time left in the day to earn more revenue from food sales. She turned to answer Eduardo's question. "How many bratwursts do you have left?"

Eduardo grinned. "Way too many."

"Sell them at half-price as a consolation," Lexi instructed.

Eduardo's face lit up. "I can do that. Good idea."

Lexi gave him her grandfather's nod and ran smack dab into the last person she wanted or expected to see—Uncle Bill. She hadn't seen his reservation on the list, so his presence caught her totally by surprise. She *needed* Roman now more than ever, but he still was nowhere to be found. Lexi fumed. First, he abandons her by not showing up for the meeting. Now this. She wasn't ready or prepared for this conversation.

Uncle Bill's gaze roamed the room like that of a lion. "Lexi, darling, this is stunning."

Terror roared through Lexi. What if he were here to add more pressure about selling his shares? Or worse, to inform her of a developer's offer? Instead of waiting for him to bring up the uncomfortable subject, she listened to her instincts and made the split-second decision to tackle it head-on.

"We did as much upgrading as we could afford with the funds left in the account, including repairs to the course."

Uncle Bill pulled out a white leather playing glove from his pocket and stretched his fingers into it. "I heard about the new signage on every tee box. What's that all about?"

"We wanted players to start each hole with words of encouragement or a bit of humor. Each hole has a hand-painted message."

"And the bench at Lookout Point?"

"Some things are worth hanging. That being one of them." He was referring, of course, to the concrete bench she couldn't part with. She wanted to keep the mementos like the old bridge and the bench in good repair.

Uncle Bill snorted. "I'm very impressed. You've been busy."

Lexi saw her opening. She wanted the upper hand when it came to the sale of his shares. It was now or never. "We decided to open the venue to small weddings." Lexi knew to expect some kickback. This was way outside the realm of their expertise.

Uncle Bill's eyes widened as he bit back a chuckle. "Weddings! Who put that crazy idea into your head? Your grandfather would never have approved of such a radical idea. I can only imagine what he would have said."

In the past, Lexi would've buckled under such opposition, but something deep inside of her had changed. It wasn't until this moment that she realized she was free. Free of the never-ending doubt, free of always worrying about failing, free of all the negative thinking that once held her back. It felt like she'd thrown the shroud of incapability off her shoulders and into the Bay waters. The years of feeling like an outsider in her own life were over. She had finally grown up and she knew exactly who she had to thank for it. Her heart skipped a beat.

With a brand-new perspective of who she was, Lexi straightened her shoulders and looked Uncle Bill square in the eyes. "I disagree. I think if Gramps had found himself in my position, with an investor looking to sell his shares, he'd have done anything in his power to retain ownership of the club. That's exactly what I plan to do."

Uncle Bill's eyebrows rose. "I'm glad to see you've become the person your grandfather always knew you would be."

Lexi smiled, but she didn't allow her thinking to be sidetracked. "Here's what I propose. I'd like to start a payment plan, where I will buy twenty-five percent of your shares today and continue purchasing every month until I have bought them all."

Uncle Bill narrowed his eyes, making it impossible for Lexi to tell if he was considering her offer. "With all the changes going on, I'm a little concerned about how you'll manage once Mr. Hart finishes his job here. I saw the sign-up sheets for league play and holiday outings and now you're adding weddings to the mix on top of everything else." He shook his head as if on the winning side of a debate team.

Lexi threw him her most confident smile. Once again, she recalled Roman's words. *It's your time.* "I can understand your concern. Roman has been invaluable.

He was the catalyst behind many of the changes that you're admiring, but the transition from the old to the new is over. I'm ready to step up and take over. Roman *was* the key, but he empowered me to take the reins of this operation, and I'm ready to stand on my own."

Lexi was so tempted to fill in the awkward silence that followed as she waited for Uncle Bill's response. Instead, she stood statue-like, in the same manner she remembered Roman doing so many times during similar situations. She was prepared to wait him out. Maybe this offer was not what he wanted, ideally, but over the years he and her grandfather had many business dealings together. Lexi knew, somewhere inside of him, that he was a reasonable man.

When he straightened up his shoulders, Lexi prepared herself for the worst and began strategizing another plan.

Uncle Bill interrupted her thoughts. "Young lady, you have yourself a deal. I'd prefer to be paid out immediately, but looking around, I can see what you've done here is nothing less than admirable. I'm willing to bet you're going to do very well for yourself, despite my concerns." He gave her a quick wink, and with that gesture, the tension between them eased considerably.

Lexi smiled. With a grateful heart, this was exactly what she'd hoped to hear. Opening her arms, she gave Uncle Bill a congenial hug. "I'll have Analise send over the agreement along with the first installment."

Uncle Bill heard his name and tee time announced. "Sounds good," he said, then threw up his hands. "And that's my tee time over…a loudspeaker?" He grinned. "Your idea?"

Lexi shook her head. "Enjoy your round." Now she

really did want to find Roman. She resumed her walk through the clubhouse and spotted Mick. Maybe he knew something of Roman's whereabouts.

"How's day one with the starter booth?" Lexi asked. After decades of knowing the man, she could tell by the determined look on his face that he was in heaven.

"I need a new stash of scorecards and pencils. This is wonderful and I'm lovin' it. The players are happy and so am I. Everything is so much more organized. I'm not scrambling in and out of the clubhouse, searching for the next group. Roman's idea for a startup booth with an intercom was right on target."

"Agreed," Lexi said. "You'll find the scorecards in the supply pantry. We have all our supplies in big plastic bins and marked with magic markers. I liked how organized the maintenance building had become so I used the same method in our supply pantry. You shouldn't have a problem finding anything."

"Thanks, Lex."

Before he headed in that direction, Lexi asked, "Hey, Mick, have you seen Roman?"

Mick's smile turned to a frown. "I think he left."

Lexi felt the blood drain from her face. "Left? What do you mean? He wouldn't do that. We've been preparing for our opening day since he first arrived."

Mick shook his head. "It was the strangest thing. He was telling me he had to go, but the look on his face," Mick waved a hand across his face, "…in his eyes. I don't know. All I can say is, he was off. You know what I mean?" Mick shrugged, clearly at a loss for words to explain the situation. "Anyway, I know you'll figure it out. You seem to know him better than any of us. Sorry I can't talk more, but I've got to get back out there. He said to tell you he left something for you in your office."

Roman left something for me? Now that definitely sounded like goodbye. Lexi gave Mick a reassuring pat on his back. "You go ahead, Mick. I'll track him down."

Ellie turned the corner, then stopped in her stride. "Lex, what is it? And don't tell me *nothing* because I can see it by the look on your face."

Lexi sighed. "The day couldn't have gone any better. We enjoyed a full day of reservations, the food service was a hit, Roman's brochures are all gone and the meeting for our first wedding went smoothly. It's Roman."

"Roman?" Ellie asked, scanning the room for him. "Where is he anyway?"

"I don't know, and I don't understand either. I thought he and I … I mean… I thought we…"

Ellie laid a hand on Lexi's arm. "Don't even begin to second guess what you have with that man. It's a beautiful start to what could be your *wonderful*. You need to find him."

"That's just it. I think he's already gone. Could I have misread the signals? Mick just told me he had something delivered for me. It's in my office."

Ellie hooked her arm in Lexi's and steered her like a mother walking her child to the first day of school. "What are we waiting for? Let's go."

Lexi gawked at the crate leaning against the wall in her office. It stood nearly as tall as she and her sister. Lexi covered her mouth with her fingers. "What on earth has he done?"

"Let's not waste any time," Ellie said. She handed Lexi the box cutter she always kept in her pocket. "I have a feeling this will answer the questions you have about

Roman."

Lexi carefully ran the blade's edge against the packing tape, splitting the seam. She paused and gave her sister a look. "You *know* what's inside?"

Ellie buttoned her lips.

Lexi huffed. "Of course, you're not talking." She flipped open the sides, and with Ellie's help, lifted a large wall portrait wrapped in bubble wrap from the box. She bent down and rested on her knees, peeling back the protective layers. Finally, she gazed into the faces of her and her grandfather. She must've been ten, maybe eleven years old. Tears welled in her eyes. "I...I don't believe what I'm looking at. How could he have managed something like this?"

"I can answer that question," Analise said, stepping into the office and the conversation. "Roman had one of his artist friends paint it from a photograph."

"But where would he get a picture of me and Gramps?"

"That's where I come in," Ellie chuckled.

Lexi should have known all along. "You two!"

"He asked both of us how we'd feel if he had the portrait made. He didn't want to exclude us but wanted to honor the relationship you had with Gramps. We all know how special it was," Ellie said.

Lexi stared at the portrait through misty eyes. Roman had given her the ultimate gift. One that she would cherish for a lifetime. "Oh, Roman," she breathed.

Analise drew close. "He thought you might want to hang it in the main dining area where it would be visible to everyone. He said some things are worth hanging onto. Your relationship with Gramps was one of them."

The exact words she'd used with him about Lookout

Point. He hadn't forgotten. "I didn't misread the signs at all, did I?"

Ellie shook her head. "No, you didn't."

Lexi wished she could wrap her arms around the portrait. "How could I think he didn't care? I was so wrong…so very wrong. I have to find him."

"I saw him leave earlier and assumed he was coming right back. Did you have a chance to check the guest cottage?" Analise asked.

"And if he's not there, use your best judgment and find the man," Ellie piped in.

Lexi's gaze moved from one sister to the other. "Really?"

"Yes, and hurry it up while you're at it. Ellie and I will close up," Analise said.

Lexi's gaze darted between her two sisters. "Are you two sure? It's been a while since you've wrapped things up here."

Ellie threw her an outrageous smile, pouring her lighthearted humor into the moment. "Absolutely, one hundred percent sure. Now go."

Lexi reached for her sisters' hands and gave them a light squeeze. "I think I know where he is."

Ellie looked at Analise and smiled. "I knew she would."

Chapter 17

Roman pulled hard on the bowling alley door. It banged with a loud slam against the exterior wall. He regretted that move instantly when heads turned in his direction and questioning glances followed. He strode into the dimly lit interior, quieting his demeanor. He had to get his head on straight and fast. Or was it his heart that was causing this blasted pain? Rolling balls down the alley always helped him solve a problem, so he was here instead of heading to his next job.

"Any open lanes?" he asked the attendant. Was it his imagination or had the employee pointed him toward lane twelve—the farthest lane at the end of the bowling hall? It didn't matter. He wasn't here to make friends. As he made his way to the shoe rental, he heard the laughter coming from other players, the balls hitting the alleys, and the pins falling. He remembered the bowling party with Lexi and the crew and how much fun he'd had. His heart took a hit. *I'm going to miss them all.*

After slipping on a pair of shoes, he surveyed the racks of bowling balls, searching for the perfect one to fit his mood. Finally, he selected the heaviest ball on the rack and slipped his two fingers and thumb into the drilled holes.

He positioned his feet directly behind the foul line. His laser-focused eyes targeted the first and third pins. He was aiming for the pocket. Roman threw his first ball. *Ah, feels good.* By the sixth frame, he was in a groove bending his patience to wait for his ball to roll back on the return. When a thin line of perspiration prickled his forehead, Roman's head cleared. This was exactly what he needed.

The day's events rewound like a movie in his head. Eduardo handled the grilling with ease, the reservations ran to sunset, and by the looks of the clipboards, two brand-new leagues had plenty of registrants signed up. So why couldn't he shake the sour mood? He threw another ball down the lane. Six pins stood standing. Hmph.

It all began when he allowed his guard to tumble down. He started caring about the golf course to meet Lexi halfway. A floodgate of emotions followed, bursting down the dam he'd so carefully constructed. It was then his feelings for Lexi began to snowball out of control.

All that didn't matter now. Lexi didn't need him. He'd overheard that plain and clear in her conversation with Bill Moros. And she was right. The job he was hired to do was done. It was painfully obvious they didn't share the same feelings for one another.

It didn't take him long to head back to the guest

cottage after what he'd heard. He'd packed up his gear and drove out of the place, virtually unseen.

The only problem was, he'd left his heart behind.

~

Taking her sister's advice, Lexi checked the guest cottage first. It looked as if he'd checked out of a hotel room. Everything was in its place but all of Roman's items were gone. Lexi jogged to her Jeep, started the engine, and headed into town, hoping she'd catch him.

She passed the hardware store and The Perfect Cup Café. No Roman. *Where is he?* Lexi's heart sped up as fast as her mind was racing. Even though she didn't think he'd be at the grocery store she included it in her search but came up empty. Finally, she discovered his truck parked in the bowling alley's parking lot. She should've known. Lexi quickly parked and slipped inside.

Choosing an inconspicuous stool at one end of the bar, Lexi ordered a coffee and scanned the area for Roman. *There he is.* She studied him. He rolled the ball down the lane with such speed, that it neared recklessness. Lexi shook her head. No wonder the attendant stuck him on alley twelve. He probably saw that train wreck of a man coming as soon as Roman walked through the door. It wasn't until he turned around that she noticed the deep-set lines on his face. She could see from her perch at the bar, that he was troubled.

He'd told her when they first met that he liked to blow off steam at the alley. It was apparent this was one of those days. Lexi slipped her bottom lip between her teeth. By the looks of the guest cottage, he intended to leave, yet, he was here. Second thoughts?

Lexi hoped so. She couldn't imagine life without him. She didn't want Roman to move on to the next job that would take him across the Midwest, away from her, but to stay in her life—forever. They needed the time to figure that out. She had to find out if he felt the same way for her as she did for him. Lexi finished her coffee, paid the tender, and walked over to Roman's lane.

Taking advantage of Roman's turned back, she quickly positioned herself behind him in the scorekeeper's chair. When he finished throwing his ball she asked, "Well, what did you end up with?" Lexi acted as if nothing was out of the ordinary and held the pen poised to hit the correct number to tally up the game.

A genuine smile spread across his face, washing away the etched torment from a moment ago. "Not the strike I wanted. What are you doing ... how did you find me?"

She rose from the chair and faced him. "I'm a good student. I listen when people talk to me. Why did you leave, Roman? We were having the best day of our lives, with a record number of reservations, the meeting with Cassie and Luke went well. Your brochures were completely gone. What happened?"

He shrugged. "It was time for me to move on. I didn't want to spoil such a perfect day for you with that kind of news. When you know, you know."

"Yet, you're here, at the bowling alley, throwing balls down the lane, as if the solution to your problem is in the next ball."

He tilted his head in the automatic way when he was challenged. "Who said I have a problem?"

"It didn't take me long to figure that out. I'd say a whole five minutes."

"I got my next assignment so I packed up my gear and started driving. I would've called and said goodbye, eventually. Somehow, I ended up here. I...I couldn't leave."

Now we're getting somewhere. "Why couldn't you leave?" Lexi held her breath waiting for Roman's answer.

Roman's eyes met hers. "It's been... so long... since I've felt this way."

Her heart picked up beats. Lexi closed in. "Then why leave at all? I still don't understand." She heard the tenderness in her voice and hoped it touched him.

Roman hesitated as if he were stumbling his way up a mountain. Lexi had never seen him so distraught. She knew she couldn't help him. He had to come to terms with what he was feeling or they'd never move forward together. He had to believe that he deserved love. That he'd been forgiven.

"I was on my way to tell you that the superintendent of schools is interested in my golf program for kids. He said there is a good chance other districts in the state might be too if the pilot program is successful. We set up a teleconference next week to get the ball rolling."

Lexi's heart lifted. "Roman, that's exactly the break you've been looking for. That's wonderful. You did it. *This* is the break you needed for your program."

Roman nodded. "It is, and I'm grateful."

Lexi rewound what Roman had just told her. "Wait a minute. You said you were on your way over to tell me?"

"I accidentally overheard your conversation with your uncle and how you explained the transition from the old to the new is over." Roman shook his head. "I'm not needed anymore. We both know that."

Lexi's shoulders fell. Now she understood. "Oh,

Roman."

Roman raised a hand, stopping her. "You're right. My job at Cherry Orchard is finished."

Lexi stepped closer. "But you're forgetting one important distinction."

Roman dragged his gaze back to look at her. Her heart ached to hold him.

"Which is?" he finally asked.

"The line between my personal life and my business. Because of you, I'm no longer hiding behind all the imaginary inadequacies anymore. I've let them all go, every last one of them but that doesn't mean I don't need you in my personal life. You're the only reason I'm standing in front of you right now. It has absolutely nothing to do with business but has everything to do with my feelings for you."

Lexi inched closer. "Now *you* have to find the same kind of strength and fight for the happiness you deserve in your life. I don't want you to leave, Roman. That is…if you feel the same way about me that I do about you."

~

Roman searched for the right words, trying to sidestep the hammering of his heart against his chest.

This is it.

He knew what he said next could change his life forever. And, oh, did he want that change.

For such a long time, he believed he had come to fix everything that was broken about Cherry Orchard. But God had other plans for him. He placed Roman exactly where he had to be to reflect, to repent, and to heal. Roman couldn't remember when he'd figured that out, but he did believe that was what brought him here. *He* needed mending more than the golf course.

With his wounds healed Roman didn't have to run from his feelings anymore. It was over. He looked at Lexi, waiting for his answer, and shook his head. "I don't want to leave. You mean the world to me. He reached for her hands and she slid hers in his. *Warm. Tender.*

"Oh, Roman. You have no idea how long I've waited to hear that. So, one step at a time?" Lexi asked, repeating their motto.

Roman smiled and pulled her closer. "One step at a time, Alexandria Russo."

Lexi gazed into his eyes, her fingers working the curls at the nape of his neck. When their lips met for the first time, Roman knew the best years of their lives lay ahead.

Chapter 18 Epilogue One Year Later

A warm summer breeze floated through Lexi's hair while sitting on the bench at Lookout Point. She would never grow tired of watching the amber rays from the setting sun melt into the Bay waters. She reached for Roman's hand. This had always been one of her favorite childhood memories of times spent with Gramps. Having Roman at her side made it all the more special. He gave her hand a gentle squeeze, telling her without words he was right where he wanted to be … home.

They had experienced nothing short of magical in the past year. The golf course became very busy, very quickly once they formed organized weekly leagues for men, ladies, and couples. Then they added scrambles and best ball events for the three holidays and the reservation book reflected a pleasantly full season. Along with the wedding bookings, they were able to swing an early buyout for Uncle Bill. To Lexi's surprise, she was now working on an outing to raise funds for the local women's shelter.

Roman tipped his head toward her. "You ready to head down for the July 4th fireworks? He kissed the soft spot on her neck.

Smiling into the twilight, she said. "I wouldn't want to miss our first public fireworks show. I bet it won't be long and our engaged couples will start asking for some kind of light show for their weddings."

Roman offered his hand and helped Lexi to her feet. "It's a nice way to put a finishing touch on the happiest day of a couple's life."

Lexi followed Roman back to the golf cart and climbed in. Even though it was still warm, he reached into the basket behind the seat, pulled out a light cotton throw, and spread it across her lap. How she loved all the little ways Roman expressed affection toward her. His concern for her wellbeing was one of the many reasons she'd fallen madly in love with him.

As they made their way back to the clubhouse, Lexi admired the star-like quality of the guided path. "I'm glad we replaced all the lights leading the way back to the clubhouse. It gives such a magical feel."

Roman navigated the cart around a bend in the path. "I prefer the word enchanting."

Lexi gave him a light push, remembering when she used the exact words on him when they'd first met. Had it really been a year ago? It was hard to believe. So much had happened between them.

Pulling into their regular stall, Roman turned off the engine and leaned forward, gazing out the front windshield. The music of crickets surrounded them. "Doesn't she look grand?" He was referring, of course, to the pet name he'd given the clubhouse.

Lexi rubbed Roman's shoulders. "The cherry apple red was the perfect color for the new paint job. And the logo Ellie handcrafted put on the finishing touch. There's not much left we have to do."

"Conrad's idea of having a view of the new gazebo, with the Bay right behind it, from your new office window was a winner. It gives the couples you meet with a perfect snapshot of all the possibilities for their wedding."

"I had my doubts about adding on the addition at the time, even though I needed a decent office, but I'm glad we decided to move forward with it and the small kitchen renovation. Now we can offer catered meals along with a food truck menu."

"Agreed. Isn't it hard to remember what the building looked like before?"

Lexi's heart filled pulled. "Not for me." She felt the warmth of Roman's hand cover hers. She understood his point, but for her, the past would always remain close to her heart. So much had changed over the past year. With the wedding side of the business exploding right along with golf reservations, Lexi turned to work almost full-time in that branch of the business, while Roman handled the course day-to-day. She hoped her grandfather would've been proud of all they'd accomplished.

Lexi nodded. "Now that we have packages couples can choose from, my job is so much easier. From the perfect setting, the dinner, and their flowers, corsages, and boutonnieres. We offer everything they need in one place. The more we can provide, the easier it is for them. And Cassie is interested in providing the breakfast items for a bridal brunch that I'd like to start offering."

Roman tilted his head to meet her gaze. "Well, haven't you become the lady entrepreneur?"

Lexi beamed in Roman's admiration. "You should talk! Having your golf program implemented in the local school district was no small feat. And now you have meetings with the private schools and a homeschool co-op."

"And I couldn't be happier. It's more than I hoped for."

"But well deserved, Roman. We make a beautiful partnership, don't we?"

Roman shook his head. "One I never saw coming."

Lexi heard the quick-witted humor in his voice. *Is he serious?* "What do you mean by that? We got along beautifully right from the start."

Roman burst into hearty laughter as they strode toward the blanketed area where they found friends and family setting up for the fireworks show. "You couldn't stand my guts and you know it." He pulled her close and tucked her under his arm. "But I wore you down, didn't I? Even made you fall in love with me."

Lexi gazed into Roman's face. He didn't have the chance to shave. His hair was blown out of place from their time on the cliff. But it was his words that caught her off guard. It was the first time he'd mentioned the word *love* between them. Oh, they felt it all right and danced on its floor of euphoria, but admitting it to one another? That hadn't come yet…or did that just happen?

Lexi lowered herself to the blanket Roman had spread out for them. She slipped off her sandals and snuggled in close to him. Placing a lightweight throw over their legs, their bare feet met somewhere underneath. Lexi smiled, content until she felt something rough rubbing against her leg.

"What on earth is going on?" Lexi screeched at the same time the first set of fireworks blew off. Red, white, and blue streaming sparkles burst into the sky and fell toward them like a rain shower.

Lexi reached for her legs while Roman gingerly poked at the blanket. "Is there a problem with the throw?"

Despite kids having fun, running around with sparklers, and teens throwing smoke bombs, Lexi didn't miss the mischief in Roman's voice. She flung the blanket to the side and found a tiny little box wedged between Roman's toes. He'd been rubbing it against her leg!

Despite her heart beating like a drum, Lexi chuckled. "Is that for me?" she asked. This was absolutely adorable and so Roman.

Roman lifted her chin so her gaze met his. It was then she saw the light of love in his eyes. "I wanted to make it original." He shrugged, looking adorable.

"It?" Lexi asked, knowing full well what Roman meant. Heart racing along with her ragged breaths, Lexi watched Roman retrieve the box and hand it to her.

She opened it with shaky hands and found a beautiful round diamond, surrounded by tiny round garnets, her birthstone. *He remembered.*

"Oh, Roman!" Lexi breathed.

She felt his warm breath on her cheek. "I love you, Lex," he whispered, "will you marry me?"

Loving Roman as much as she did, Lexi hadn't realized how long she'd been waiting for this moment. She gazed lovingly into his smiling face. "In a heartbeat," she murmured.

Christine A. Schimpf

His smile lit up the dark sky and Lexi knew they had each found their way home in each other.

Roman slipped the engagement ring on Lexi's finger. "I can't think of a better way to end the evening he said and kissed her softly on her lips just as the next set of boom, boom, boom fireworks exploded overhead.

www.ingramcontent.com/pod-product-compliance
Lightning Source LLC
LaVergne TN
LVHW010330070526
838199LV00065B/5713